WELCOME HONORABLE VISITORS

WELCOME
HONORABLE
VISITORS

A novel by JEAN RASPAIL

Translated by Jean Stewart

G. P. PUTNAM'S SONS
New York

Contents

WELCOME HONORABLE VISITORS

I

Mr. Miyamoto and Some Others

Mr. Miyamoto—Miyamoto San—was jubilant. Needless to say, his face betrayed no hint of joy. Indeed, an uninformed Western observer might have supposed that this twenty-four-year-old student was hurrying to his mother's deathbed, and that the gleam in his dark eyes was the wild light of heartbreak. By no means. Mr. Miyamoto, as he tramped the wet pavement of Tokyo that evening, was profoundly happy. His train of thought moved him, now and then, to utter noncommittal grunts, interspersed with exclamations, like a pot on the boil emitting an occasional puff of steam; nobody took any notice, so natural do the Japanese find it to hear another Japanese grunting.

Above all, Mr. Miyamoto was feeling proud. His heart swelled as he thought of the confidence placed in him by that honorable foreigner from the Marunuchi Hotel, whom he had met for the first time ten days previously. The contract had been made through the employment columns of the English edition of the *Japanese Times*:

> Director of French Travel Agency "Unknown Lands" seeks enterprising young Japanese, speaking French or English, with some knowledge of Western ways, to act as guide to tourists during one month's stay Tokyo. Apply M. Gilles Germain, Marunuchi Hotel, Tokyo, any evening between 5 and 7.

Miyamoto, an assiduous fan of all the French films shown in Tokyo, had judged himself sufficiently familiar with Western ways to answer M. Germain's appeal. He was not alone in so doing; on the day he chose, he found a score of other Japanese in the lobby of the Marunuchi Hotel, waiting to be interviewed. Fifteen of these, sprawling on the leather armchairs, were chewing gum or smoking Lucky Strikes, specially bought at great expense from the hotel stall. The *Japanese Times* peeped from their pockets. Their knowledge of Western ways, as required by the advertisement, had inspired them to go American, and they did so brazenly, thanks to that gift of involuntary and somewhat simian mimicry which is the birthright of every Japanese. Some of them had even gone so far as to procure the weekly edition of *The New York Times*. One shrewd little fellow flaunted the *Christian Science Monitor*, on the grounds that what appealed to Americans was bound to appeal to the French. The five remaining candidates had chosen to look artistic, assuming that open-necked shirts, corduroy trousers and Basque berets, particularly Basque berets like Utrillo's, would convince M. Germain that they were practically his compatriots. These five were smoking pipes and coughing loudly. All of them felt very Western, especially those who had taken the precaution of acquiring dark glasses. Not one of them considered himself in fancy dress, although they had spent their last yen that very morning buying accessories—pipes, newspapers, Lucky Strikes and Basque berets. Mr. Miyamoto, who spoke French correctly and English more or less, had not given a thought to his appearance.

When it came to his turn to be ushered into M. Germain's room, he had made a very low Japanese bow. He was never to realize that it was this orthodox salutation which won him the favor of the Frenchman, who was weary of all the hearty Western handshakes offered by the other candidates. Germain was after local color, and he wanted a Japanese, not one of the bogus GIs or pseudo art students who had been parading through his room for the past two hours. Mr. Miyamoto, somewhat ashamed of his skimpy suit, his close-shaven head and the wet umbrella which, in his excitement, he had forgotten to leave in the cloakroom, had been subjected to a long scrutiny. At last, here's a Jap who looks like a Jap! Germain had told himself. And he had engaged the little man on the spot.

In Germain's company Mr. Miyamoto had lived through an extraordinary week: lunches and dinners in European restaurants, with endless meat dishes that tried his rice-accustomed stomach, colloquies with important personalities whom he gradually learned to treat on an equal footing, as Germain did—a source of supreme satisfaction in a country where the social ladder comprises ninety million rungs—and finally the astonishing experience of seeing Germain received at the French Embassy without waiting, and securing in five minutes letters of introduction which Japanese officialdom at its most efficient would have taken a week to grant. Now he rejoiced in the title of Assistant to the Director, and his admiration for his boss knew no bounds.

That evening, as he trudged incognito through the crowded streets of Tokyo, Mr. Miyamoto gloated once again over his good fortune. What an achievement, what an honor to be chosen from among so many candidates for so responsible a post! Tomorrow he would go and tell his friends, Mr. Kishi and Mr. Kondo, about this feather in his cap; they'd be certain to congratulate him heartily, although he was fully aware of his own unworthiness.

He stopped short, staring vacantly ahead, and pondered. Five passers-by jostled him, an old woman trod on his foot, and a dignitary spat on his trousers; and yet he did not take offense.

He was faced with a grave problem of etiquette: if he were to go the very next day to tell his friends the good news, his haste might suggest vanity, and moreover might hurt their feelings, since they had been chasing lucrative jobs for so long without success. But if he didn't go, they were liable to learn of his recent promotion from somebody else, and then they would be obliged to pay him a congratulatory visit themselves, and that would be very bad form on his part. A most awkward situation! Really, the safest course was to put the problem to Uncle Yasui San, an authority on questions of etiquette, thanks to twenty years' experience of dealing with knotty problems while in charge of the Ginza Subway Station. He would take a small gift to his uncle, of course.

Mr. Miyamoto started off again, then halted almost immediately. Yes, of course, but . . . he would also have to tell his uncle about the confidential post he had been given, and Uncle would think it most discourteous of so important a nephew to bring only a small gift. What, then? Two bottles of sake, for instance? No. Two bottles of sake would be too much for Uncle Yasui, who did not earn the wherewithal to buy them for himself, still less to repay his present with one of equal value on the next occasion. One bottle of sake then, which they could drink quietly while they discussed the honorable stranger and his highly instructive eccentricities. Sake was a first-rate idea, particularly as old Aunt Yasui would be there to pour it out; she'd take in every word of the conversation, and in a couple of days most of the women in the family would be acquainted with the honor fallen to the student Miyamoto San. The news would spread swiftly from the women to the men, and would raise his prestige to a level with that of the Stationmaster himself, or his little cousin the Police Sergeant, the two dignitaries of the Miyamoto clan.

Mr. Miyamoto walked twenty yards, stared at a couple of women, and then stopped short again. Such a reputation would bring visitors to see him, probably more visitors than on the day when his photograph had appeared on Page 20 of the *Mainichi*, above a small literary piece he had written on Fencing in the Work of Alexandre Dumas, with the accompanying words: *Miyamoto San, one of the youngest and most eminent of Japanese authorities on Alexandre Dumas.* But in the main room of his home, the same *kakemono* had been hanging for the past two years on the *tokonoma* wall, whereas good taste required that they should be changed from time to time. Miyamoto San had had to sell all his, except this one, to pay his mother's hospital bill. His father, a general in the Army of the Rising Sun, had committed suicide at the end of the war in an obscure corner of the Kuril Islands, and money was scarce for ex-officers' families. But now that times had changed, it would be against all the rules of decorum for visitors to be confronted with the same *kakemono* that they had already seen two years before. And his relatives had good memories, particularly old Aunt Yasui! To be sure, she would say as she congratulated him: "How wise of you to have kept that precious *kakemono*, I've never seen a more attractive one!" She would say this in all sincerity, but, like a good Japanese, he would realize that this comment, particularly if sincerely spoken, meant exactly the opposite, and he could not endure such an affront.

That very evening he would change the *kakemono*.

Having thus pruned the complex tangle of his social preoccupations, Mr. Miyamoto darted off through the falling dusk, unaware of the rain streaming over the frayed edges of his old umbrella and seeping unpleasantly through the worn soles of his shoes. He hurriedly bought a small bag of sliced dried octopus, his favorite delicacy, and nibbled it nervously as he went his way.

All around him Tokyo was lighting up, and the many-colored neon lights on its huge street signs proclaimed his country's greatness. Mr. Miyamoto's thoughts went soaring up . . . He was a law student already, practically a doctor of law, he was a great authority on Alexandre Dumas and was now preparing a subtle thesis on the Use of Adverbs in the work of George Sand; he was going to take advantage of his new situation to produce a psychological study of the behavior of Western tourists, a study which would make him famous, without a shadow of doubt, and win him the coveted title of *Sensei*, Master. A *sensei* at twenty-five! With his soul in a ferment, he darted into one of those modern coffee houses which abound in Tokyo, and where for a hundred yen you can get bad coffee and good classical music. For an hour he sat there bolt upright, open-mouthed, staring, in an ecstasy, listening to Beethoven and beating time, and dreamed he was signing thousands of autographs, doubly famous as conductor and as author.

The record stopped and the last note of the Fifth Symphony brought the great writer back with a jerk to his *kakemono*. Simultaneously, twenty other young Japanese came down to earth. Carried away by the music, they had imagined themselves fashionable painters, famous actors, baseball stars, senators, rich businessmen, professors or great scientists. . . . Having paid their hundred yen, they put on their black student caps again and went out in silence. Some of them made their way toward the flickering lamps of the open-air stalls of the *soba* sellers, those little restaurants on wheels that feed thousands of worthy citizens of Tokyo. For fifty yen they could get noodle soup and a bowl of rice, which they would swallow standing there in the rain, with much flicking of chopsticks and a noise like ducks drinking. Having cheated hunger, they would hurry off to their night work to earn, through long sleepless hours, the three hundred yen that would ensure their next day's survival. It didn't matter, they would sleep later, in the morning, on the streetcar carrying them to the University, where they would sway, close-packed, among that throng of weary, drowsy, ill-fed travelers with faces more green than yellow which is one of the saddest sights in Tokyo. Others would go off to join their friends for one of those arduous all-night discussions that young Japanese delight in: human nature, life, love, beauty, Peace. The future of Japan would be examined conscientiously, gravely, but without any ideas other than those derived from books. They would fling in one another's faces, exultantly, Pascal, Kant, Marx, Sartre,

14

Faulkner, Malraux and so forth, and never take a step forward. Poor Japanese! Hampered by the complexity of their language, their brains painfully crammed with that crazy script of several thousand Chinese characters that don't even correspond to their own tongue, fettered by the world's most punctilious formalism, they tackle the great questions of modern life armed with these boomerangs! Progress has come from the West, but although the whole world has adopted it, only the West, which invented it, has so far proved capable of extracting a moral code from it, of discovering its philosophy. And the poor little Nipponese, bound fast in his network of anachronisms and superstitions like a mummy in its wrappings, tries in vain, with aching head, to fit a Japanese meaning to modern life.

Take a quick look at that student who left the coffee house shortly before Miyamoto San, and whose thin melancholy figure is just about to disappear round the street corner. He had spent three hours listening to Bach, Beethoven and Mozart. But while others daydreamed, he had come there to forget. Born in a *tokushu buraky,* a special pariah village, he belonged to the caste of the impure, the *eta;* and he would bear the taint all his life. Once, in the Japanese senate, half the senators left the hall when an *eta* was spotted among the newly elected members. At school the impure were inevitably relegated to the bottom of the class; in battle they were placed in the front line and sent on suicidal missions. Since solid restrictions reduced them to intermarriage their stock was degenerating. This medieval ostracism was applied to them because their ancestors had been Korean prisoners condemned to the most menial tasks, or else slaughterers of oxen or swine, which Buddhism forbade.

And even today, when every Japanese eats meat whenever he can afford it, butchers (and shoemakers as well) are still considered impure and are kept on the fringe of society. Every large town has, in its suburbs, a special village where thousands of outcasts lead a wretched existence. A few years earlier this student, then a schoolboy, had rebelled after his own fashion. He had written in his exercise book: *Come and sow in our fields, the flowers do not refuse to bloom there. In our village peach blossom and plum blossom are no less fair than elsewhere, the peach trees do not bear plums there nor the plum trees peaches . . . And men are no different there either, so why treat them as pariahs?* The teacher had not deigned to answer, nor to modify his distant attitude. Later on at the University the student had mingled with the crowd of his fellows and his outcast state had seemed forgotten at last. He had loved a girl, and she had returned his love. But a few days ago some kindly soul had warned her; since then she had not spoken a word to him. And this evening the student was alone, once more, as he would be on all the evenings to come. . . .

Mr. Miyamoto took a deep breath of fresh air. On the doorstep of the coffee house he stretched his tiny frame and thrust his chin back and forth, to right and left, meticulously and repeatedly, to relax his stiffened muscles. This is a kind of national tic, and when, in bus or train, in your hotel or on the street, you see a Japanese twitching with an air of costive concentration, there's nothing to worry about; he is merely trying to relax. Mr. Miyamoto stepped out energetically to look for a *kakemono* shop. He fingered, in his pocket, the ten thousand-yen notes which the honorable foreigner had paid him in advance. He'd said good-by to all those financial worries which beset worthy folk such as his friends Mr. Kishi and Mr. Kondo. Henceforward the road opened out before him, sinuous and twisted as a labyrinth, bristling with complex obstacles and pitfalls of protocol consistent with his dignity, the sort of road every Japanese loves to tread, whereas the hopelessly straight line of trivial everyday problems fills his soul with confusion and uncertainty.

A few streets farther on, Mr. Miyamoto stopped short in front of a visiting-card printer's. This character is, together with the jacket renter, the confectioner and the *furoshiki* seller, one of the indispensable pillars of Japanese social life, one of those cardinal points without which the earth would stop turning. At a wedding, for instance, the guest must wear a special black jacket, comically short and skimpy; his wife must carry a box of bean-flour candies, its ribbon tied in an elaborate bow expressive of countless kind thoughts and good wishes. The box itself will be wrapped in the bright-colored square of cloth or silk called a *furoshiki*, carefully chosen by the guest's wife after half an hour of animated discussion with the salesgirl. Now it would be in the worst of taste to fold up the *furoshiki* and put it back in one's pocket. It is given with the present, and whereas the present must of course be proportionate to the wealth of the recipient, the donor can give free reign to his generosity when choosing the *furoshiki*. It is not uncommon to see a hundred-yen worth of candy wrapped up in a *furoshiki* worth three thousand. When he has presented his gift, the guest receives, in his turn, in token of deepest gratitude, a similar box, so that he can go home and eat exactly the same candies as those he has just given. At the end of the ceremony he will exchange visiting cards with all the guests present whom he does not know. This exercise is accompanied by bows, of which by the end of the day he may well have made two or three hundred. Without its jackets, its confectionery, its visiting cards, its *furoshiki* and its polite bows, the Japanese façade would crumble.

Ordering visiting cards is usually a quick and straightforward business. But Mr. Miyamoto was anxious to do it properly. The printer, squatting on his straw mat, was warming his finger tips with a dignified air over a big pot in which three lumps of charcoal were feebly glowing. Mr. Miyamoto got down to business in Japanese fashion:

"A friend has told me about your honorable printing press and the high quality of work for which it is renowned."

Now Mr. Miyamoto had never heard of this shop before. And yet he was being perfectly sincere, observing by instinct two vital rules of decorum.

First, never broach the subject of conversation without leading up to it carefully and long-windedly. Western visitors in Japan are constantly running into trouble through neglect of this commandment. Thus you must never, as one tourist did, say to your maid point-blank: "Will you call and ask the masseur to come at five o'clock this evening?" Such an order would upset the poor girl who, taken aback by your sudden decision, runs the risk of losing face. As you wish her no harm, you go about things as follows: "I feel rather tired this evening." *Poor gentleman,* thinks the maid, as the idea sinks in, *he's so tired!* "Maybe a massage might relieve me?" *Why yes,* she reflects, beginning to understand, *massage is often a great help.* "I've still a lot of work to do tonight." *He has so much work, but how will he manage if he's so tired?* "Suppose I asked the masseur to come?" *Why of course, it's obvious,* it suddenly dawns on her. "Then please be kind enough to call him." She'll fly to the telephone. You see how easy it was?

Secondly, always arrange to be introduced by a third person. Individuality is nonexistent in Japan. Everybody is a fraction, an infinitely interchangeable molecule, an imperceptible particle exactly like ninety million other particles, which must amalgamate with others in order to acquire a certain consistency and to rise from its state of nonentity.

The printer nodded twenty times in silence, which gave him time to ponder his reply, and finally said politely, drawing out his syllables,

"Aaa . . . Aaaaaaa . . . Aaaaaaaaaah!"

He had wondered for a moment whether he ought to protest to this stranger, who had been sent him by a friend, that his wretched house was unworthy to receive so august a visitor. But that is a formula reserved for regular customers who fully appreciate your establishment. To greet a stranger thus was liable to betray an unseemly and out-of-place boastfulness. The answer he chose to give, however, was perfect, and his "aaaaaah" was emphatic enough to express a respectful and co-operative interest. Having spoken, he waited.

Mr. Miyamoto, who had not failed to grasp this nuance, went on, "I am the unworthy colleague of an important French travel agent. Although I am quite unfit for the post, owing to my deplorable ignorance of the French language, I took up my duties a few days ago."

Oho, thought the printer, so there's a foreigner involved! He leaned his head to one side and sucked in air sharply through the corner of his lips with a noise like a siphon, signs of intense perplexity in Japan. In other times he might have informed the police immediately, but nowadays the wind was blowing from the West. Be prudent, was his conclusion (till the end of the war he had been a fanatic anti-foreigner, like all his compatriots); be prudent, but polite:

"Aaaaaaa . . . So *deska* . . . really, is that so?"

The printer was being very helpful; Mr. Miyamoto was fully conscious of it. Thus authorized to go on, he launched into a long description of Gilles Germain, telling how he had taken the plane in Paris, called at Rome, Istanbul, Teheran, Karachi, Bangkok, Saigon and Manila and arrived at Tokyo in fine weather. How splendid the plane had looked, glittering in the sunshine, and how faultless was the running of the Tokyo airport! He described Germain's pleasant manners, the color of his suits and shoes, the number of letters he received every day, the bathroom of his hotel, and mentioned confidentially that he smoked Japanese cigarettes but drank black tea, with sugar.

"Aaaaaaa . . . So *deska*," said the printer who appreciated the significance of these revelations.

At this stage of the conversation, let us note two important facts. Mr. Miyamoto had been speaking for a quarter of an hour without mentioning the object of his call, which may seem pointless for somebody who is merely ordering visiting cards. But this is nothing compared to the remarkable delicacy of the businessman who, wanting to buy five tons of nickel, wrote two unforgettable pages about cherry trees in bloom and the beauty of Nature in April. At the end of the letter, in a couple of lines, as though it were a superfluous detail, he expressed his wish to receive five tons of nickel as soon as possible, and then closed with some reflections on the temperature. As for the printer, he had held his part in the duet extremely well, and it was not so easy. By dint of saying *Aaaa so deska* with a great variety of intonations, he managed to convey the prodigious interest he took in his visitor, without overstepping the bounds of a seemly reserve. Indeed, if he had had other problems to worry over, he could have thought about them quite peacefully during the course of Mr. Miyamoto's story, for the Japanese brain is well adapted to that kind of duplicity.

". . . And thus," Mr. Miyamoto concluded, "it appears to me essential for the proper exercise of my new functions to beg you for five hundred visiting cards."

"Excuse my utter incompetency," replied the printer, who had practiced the trade for thirty years. "I will do my best."

The inscription for the card was drawn up as follows:

K. MIYAMOTO
Assistant to the Director, French Travel Agency
"Unknown lands"

This appeared on the French side. The reverse was written in Japanese and ran from top to bottom and from right to left. The printer copied out the formula and showed it to Mr. Miyamoto, who approved it, apologized for various lapses of etiquette, and withdrew. He had taken a great step forward in life.

The *kakemono* was soon bought. Mr. Miyamoto knew just what he wanted, something sober and bare, according to the curiously contradictory taste of his compatriots, who like to rest from their painfully complicated mental processes by gazing, at home, at objects so simple as to be almost nonexistent. The sight of a neutral-tinted cup with a slightly irregular brim, for example, transports a Japanese to ecstasy. A single daisy, standing upright in an earthenware pot, will call forth cries of admiration. At the theatre he will squat on his heels for an entire evening to hear the actors in a *no* play spin out for whole quarters of an hour, syllable by syllable, remarks which, uttered normally, would take about two minutes. Mr. Miyamoto, giving vent to his secret longing for simplicity, chose a print which, from afar, looked like a virgin sheet of gray paper. Closer examination, however, revealed in the lower left-hand corner a wild flower suggested in four delicate brush strokes, and in the top right-hand corner a tiny cloud which almost merged into the background paper. He carried it off in a roll under his arm, with great satisfaction, convinced that this subtle sketch would make a most favorable impression on his visitors.

Thus protected on every side, Mr. Miyamoto took the bus home.

At the same time, the ex-lieutenant Hakayama San was preparing to leave the portal of the Yasukuni Temple, where he had been stationed since eight o'clock that morning. The stump of his knee was aching, and his leather hand, carrying a beggar's bowl, felt very heavy. His white tunic, the uniform of a disabled soldier, was soaked with the day's continuous rains and clung to his body. He was shivering. A score of visitors passed by. They were youngsters who had grown up in air raids and were hardened against pity—or rather against memory, since pity is a feeling unknown to the Japanese. He went through the motions of his calling, however, and bowed low, unsteadily balanced on one metal leg and one of flesh and blood. No clinking of coins repaid his gesture. The young have forgotten, thought the ex-lieutenant, that Japan once owed its power and its glory to the valor of its soldiers. He counted his takings: three hundred and ten yen, after ten hours on duty. A meager harvest! And yet the post was a good one, among the best in Tokyo, used by all the ex-service beggars in rotation. The sight of smashed faces, iron legs, leather arms, surgical stays, wooden feet, crutches, empty eye sockets, ought to have aroused the compassion of passers-by at Yasukuni of all places. For in that temple thousands of black and gold tablets were aligned, commemorating the soldiers who had died on all the battlefields of Asia, the Emperor's name on their lips. The Shinto religion made gods of them, *kami*, and the temple of Yasukuni is dedicated to them. Although defeat has diminished the veneration of the Japanese for their dead warriors, many visitors still cross the threshold of the temple. But if they respect dead gods, they look with indifference, even with hostility, at vanquished victims.

With his single eye, Hakayama San kept a sharp lookout for potential benefactors. He noticed an American officer with his camera slung around him. The conquerors were said to be generous, as every beggar knew. He bowed to the ground. The bowl remained silent. He raised his body slightly and then bowed again. Still nothing. Puzzled, he lifted his head.

"O.K., Suzuki, don't move!" The Kodak was trained on him, and the American pressed the trigger.

"Nice shot, eh, Suzuki!"

Delighted, the Amercan fumbled in his pocket and came up with a hundred-yen note in his outstretched hand. He let the hand drop in amazement; the ex-lieutenant had turned his back, rejecting the handsomest offering of the whole day.

Hakayama San made his way to the bus stop as fast as his crutch would let him. Two full buses passed; when the third came he managed to edge his way into the crowded aisle. Nobody took any notice of him. He remained standing; every jerk of the brakes sent a stab of pain through his stump. Youngsters were sleeping on the seats around him, and he longed to do likewise. An endless half-hour passed. At the far end of the aisle an old woman was sitting with a baby fastened onto her back with a great shawl. She was asleep too, when a sudden jolt woke her. She noticed the cripple and offered him her seat with a bow. The war, which had left her as sole survivor, with her daughter and grandson, of a large family, would only end, for her, with her own life. She still observed its rules and honored its victims as, twelve years earlier, the entire Japanese nation had done. Hakayama San sat down without thanking her.

He got off at the terminus, walked to the station and onto the crowded platform. He knew that, as on every other night, he would not be allowed to go in front. The loud-speaker, with the usual fine phrases, warned the honorable travelers that their train, a fast suburban train, was approaching the station. As soon as the gates opened, thousands of honorable travelers launched their attack with an impetuous ardor that the world's armies might well envy; nothing was lacking but yells of "banzai." Forgotten, now, were bows and visiting cards, smiles and compliments; Japanese politeness is merely a conventional garment, quickly discarded in favor of freedom of movement. A disorderly struggle arose between the outgoing and incoming travelers. One little old man who wanted to get off was pushed back by the tide into the middle of the car; he'd have to try again at the next station. At last the crowd assumed some sort of order, precedence being determined, according to the rules of Japanese collective politeness, by the relative weight and energy of individuals: 1) well-nourished youths, 2) men, 3) girls of every description, and undernourished youths, 4) women possessing umbrellas or parasols, knobbly parcels or sharp elbows, 5) invalids too weak to struggle, 6) mothers with small babies, 7) toddlers and women seven months pregnant, 8) old people, and finally, all alone, Hakayama San the cripple.

Hakayama San stood in discomfort for an hour, till the train stopped at his remote suburb. Outside the station he bought, for a hundred yen, a bottle of inferior sake. When he got home to the minute room which he shared with five other beggars, he knelt down on the mat. He bowed in the direction of the Imperial Palace, paying homage to the Emperor as, in old days, thousands of Japanese soldiers had done in every corner of Asia.

Then he uncorked the bottle and began to drink.

Miss Cloudless Sky, a geisha of the first class, was kneeling before her dressing table. As usual, that afternoon, she was preparing to have supper with wealthy gentlemen who would pay handsomely for her presence. She had a lively wit and was a skilled player on the samisen, and she was the mainstay of her owner, Mama San. Her black hair, carefully oiled and lacquered into stiffness, covered her head like a faultless wig. Mama San dipped a broad flat paintbrush into a small basin filled with a thin white paste. She daubed it over the girl's throat and the back of her neck, a good way down her spine, and then spread it with a shaving brush. Miss Cloudless Sky took the paintbrush herself and painted a smooth coat of white over her whole face, fore-head, eyelids and mouth. In another small dish she thinned out some rouge and colored her forehead, eyelids and cheekbones. She chose another paintbrush, sucked it with great deliberation and removed the white from her eyebrows, which she then blackened with a third brush. Then she curled her lashes with grease and painted her thin lips into a round scarlet mouth con-trasting violently with the whiteness of her face.

"You're lovelier than ever," Mama San told her. "You're cer-tain to please the honorable Minister who is giving the party."

Her make-up completed, she rose and slipped on a red under-kimono with white flowers, cut low in the back and held together in front by a broad sash fastened across the bosom. Two stoles, one white and the other richly embroidered, framed her white back charmingly. Western women show their legs, Balinese women their bosoms, Chinese women their thighs. Japanese women have bowlegs, flat bosoms and short thighs, so they show the upper part of their backs. Since the war, it must be observed, legs are growing straighter, busts fuller and thighs longer; but for full-dress kimonos, décolleté backs are still fashionable. Gen-tlemen peer down them with rapture.

Realizing what a godsend the favors of a Minister might be, Mama San chose for her geisha a kimono of sky-blue silk thickly embroidered with birds and flowers. The price of this costly work of art, three thundred thousand yen, would be charged to the geisha's account and would have to be paid for out of her earn-ings. Mama San, when she bought it, had done a good stroke of business, setting off the charms of her protégée and at the same time postponing the day when the geisha, having paid all her debts, could fly with her own wings.

Some girls never live to see that day, so onerous is the burden of debt: the sum advanced to the parents for the purchase of the geisha as a child of twelve, her board and lodging, fees for lessons in dancing and deportment, music, conversation, etc.; not to mention Mama San's well-earned profits. The only hope of early escape for a geisha lies in taking the fancy of a millionaire who will buy her back from her proprietress and set her up for his personal satisfaction in a pretty house, with the official title of "second wife." Such opportunities are growing rarer in postwar Japan, for if the law allows staggering bills for "geisha parties," sometimes up to a million yen, to be put down to expense accounts, it is still not possible to write off the purchase of a second wife.

Miss Cloudless Sky, like others of her sort, was quite satisfied with her lot. She would willingly have died for Mama San, without whose help she might still have been stagnating in her village, a wretched little peasant in baggy trousers and straw sandals, doomed to a lifetime of poverty and semislavery. Instead of which, she enjoyed a luxurious existence, full of music and dancing, laughter and delicate suppers, wonderful kimonos and jewels, free from cares and regrets, free even from thoughts: a butterfly girl, living only for the passing moment.

At the sight of the blue kimono which she had never worn, Miss Cloudless Sky clapped her hands. Bred in luxury, aware of the cost of this enchanting garment, she knew that it added to the weight of the gilded chains that bound her, but she did not care. Her heart high, she put it on ceremoniously, like a sacred vestment. Mama San brought the gold-threaded obi, the broad sash four or five yards long, and began the delicate operation of arranging it, first winding it round her from hips to armpits in a tight scarlet band, flattening the bosom. Then a little pad was placed in the small of the back and a brass frame over the stomach, to bear the weight of the obi and give it its classic shape. The process took a full quarter of an hour, and Mama San needed all her skill and knowledge to achieve the correct result.

Miss Cloudless Sky squealed with delight, and decided immediately to try out the effect of her costume on the neighboring streets. It was five o'clock in the evening, the time when the butterfly girls of the geisha district take the air before adjourning to the honorable teahouses. She put on high clogs of black lacquer, exquisite but uncomfortable, and tottered down the three steps of the porch with Mama San's assistance. With tiny slithering steps, dragging her feet, her knees slightly bent but her back and head held stiffly upright, she tripped along the lane of little wooden houses. Tittering behind her hand, a sign of intense emotion, she acknowledged her friends' compliments and then came fluttering back to the porch where Mama San awaited her. The blue butterfly had completed its flight.

At the expected time, a glittering Cadillac sent by the Minister stopped at her door. Two other geishas were already in it. Miss Cloudless Sky climbed in, smiled back at Mama San, greeted her companions and settled down. The Cadillac roared mightily and sped off in a whirl of dust.

Miss Cloudless Sky, sitting very straight so as not to disturb her coiffure, stroked the warm silky cushions with her hand, savoring the passing moment.

At five o'clock that evening, as usual, Japan reverted to its past. The Ginza, with its huge glittering street signs and its brightly lit shop windows, tried to keep its modern atmosphere, but everywhere else, as inexorable as the turn of the tides, the metamorphosis took place. In thousands of dark lanes, paper lanterns pierced the gloom with many-colored pin points of light. Hato San, the wandering soothsayer who told the fortunes of a whole neighborhood by reading hands or studying pieces of reed, lit the candle over his tiny stall. The storyteller, the *soba* seller, the paper window mender, the basketmaker, the pea vendor, the public scribe who paints *kanji*, and thousands of other barrow-pushers lit their lanterns and broadcast the strident notes of their flutes through the town. The blue-frocked minstrel set off, guitar in hand, for his round of the sake houses. Nakagawa San, a local physician, halted before a tiny open-air altar in the recess of a house wall, dedicated to Hinari the fox, messenger of the gods. He lit a stick of incense, offered up a few grains of rice, clapped his hands three times and made a deep bow. Matsuko San, who sold cameras, feeling tired, bought two grams of powdered viper from a Chinese chemist and swallowed it promptly. Koyama San, manager of an adding-machine factory, had his palm read by Hato San the soothsayer and waited for the verdict with beating heart. Sato San, a high police official, put on a pilgrim's cloak and set off on foot with a sort of rattle in his hand. He spent every evening praying in a different Buddhist temple. Takashi San ordered the maid to prepare supper for his son, who had died two years ago that very day. Keiko San, Mr. Miyamoto's young sister, readied the house for her brother's return. She laid four small pieces of charcoal in the *hibachi*, brought glowing embers between two sticks and blew to light her fire. Then she went into the "bathroom" and thrust a few logs into a stove under a great wooden bucket filled with water, to heat the *o furo*.

Millions of Japanese who had worked all day in Western fashion, sitting at their desks or standing behind their machines, from the metal worker to the Company Director, carried out precisely the same sequence of gestures. On the threshold of their homes, they changed their shoes for slippers and went indoors. Discarding the slippers outside the bedroom door they stepped in stocking feet onto the mat, and performed the daily ritual of casting off all their Western trappings, trousers and jacket, shirt and tie, which they shut up in a cupboard out of sight. Then, clad in the traditional *dotera*, a padded indoor kimono, dark colored and wide-sleeved, held tight just below the waist by a narrow belt, they changed their socks for *tabi* and, thus transformed into a Japanese print, they knelt down on the mat.

There, hands outstretched over their *hibachi*, in silent reverie, millions of Nipponese warmed their finger tips. . . .

Japan was changing its skin.

II

Vigils

———

Gilles Germain still had six hours to spare before the arrival at Tokyo Airport of the party of tourists visiting The Land of the Rising Sun under the auspices of the travel agency he had been successfully running for the past few years. Through the window of his bedroom he stared at the dense slanting rain that lashed the high walls of the Marunuchi Hotel. Really, he thought, the national flag is the only spot in the whole of Japan where that famous sun ever shines! He laughed softly. Land of the rising sun! What an atmosphere of clear and smiling radiance, of triumphant happiness, that seductive phrase suggested! He had chosen it himself. His long experience of organizing travel had taught him to picture the world as his potential patrons would like it to be. He knew the value of a certain number of basic clichés, some of which still bore a faint resemblance to the truth they had once conveyed, clichés to which most people stubbornly cling like a sick man to the hope of recovery. Thus Bali meant bare-bosomed women; Canada, trappers and Indians; Peru, the gold of the Conquistadores; India, yogis and rajahs; Mexico, bandits and revolutions; Australia, boomerangs and kangaroos. When planning a new tour, he first concocted a startling title, usually as suggestive as it was meaningless. He used to say, cyni-

29

cally: "Give a tour a good name, even if the rest of it's bad!" Next he would choose his clients according to their tastes, which were all entered in his files—a hand-picked group, all acquired through personal contacts; people with substantial bank balances, whom he looked after with realistic shrewdness like a portfolio of sound securities. Finally he went off, a month in advance, to prepare for his tourists' visit.

A messenger brought him a thick envelope sent by the director of the Japanese Travel Agency. Germain opened it and drew forth a score of photographs which he spread out on the table—the tourist's dream of Japan in glorious technicolor! Temples, dolls, arched bridges, Buddhas, flower arrangements, more temples and more arched bridges, red *tori* and stone lanterns, flowers, *tori* and temples! It's much too beautiful, he thought. Those touched-up colors, this pretentious photography, this orgy of famous beauty spots, made him feel sick. How can anyone believe for a moment that Japan is really like these pictures? He had visited all the famous spots with care, like the conscientious travel agent that he was. The first he saw he thought pretty, the second he thought pretty too but almost exactly like the first. By the twentieth he was fed up and broke off the experiment, which was particularly inconclusive in that to go from one place to another you had, each time, to cross the whole breadth of Tokyo, the black monotonous squalor of which appalled you and overwhelmed you with deepest melancholy. During the month he had spent here, Germain had come to realize that only the countryside and its tiny villages correspond to the foreigner's conception of Japan.

Now a tourist never has the leisure and rarely has the inclination to wander through the countryside, walking for long hours along a narrow road to reach some neglected hamlet which will display for him the charms of the past. Being pressed for time, he will never be able to escape from the hideousness of the towns, from the poverty of their teeming crowds, from the depressing sameness of the setting and the people. And the tourist is disappointed; he has come from the other end of the earth, to see geisha girls, cherry trees in bloom, smiling *musmes*, kimonos, polite little men, paper houses, parasols, Japanese gardens and prints. This list of clichés had been noted down by Germain, after an inquiry among his clients, as a campaign plan, and he had decided that it was the finest statement of commonplaces ever made. But for the six rich tourists who were to land at midnight that night these clichés meant something, and indeed formed the sole purpose of their visit. Germain had done his best to satisfy them, to give them the feeling of strangeness, to surround them from the moment of landing at the Tokyo airport with that typically Japanese atmosphere which they anticipated. He remembered the romantic Japanese inn which he and Miyamoto had chosen for their guests to stay at, and decided, to his satisfaction, that it would exactly answer their wishes. He shrugged his shoulders: after all, perhaps this really was Japan?

He was well acquainted with the six travelers who, at this moment, were in the air somewhere above Formosa: the soundest securities on his agency's list, people for whom money did not count, who went on two or three tours each year. A couple of months earlier, four of them had visited Kashmir, thanks to Gilles and his agency. The tour had been called: "Adventure in Kashmir." It had been a signal success; they had enjoyed a feast of adventures and came back delightedly clamoring for more. Germain had anticipated everything, and had rented the summer residence of a down-and-out rajah for ten days. For five million francs he got not only the palace but also the Rajah's five Sikh warriors, his three dancing girls, his ten servants and his black slave, not to mention three elephants, two elephant keepers, and the Rajah himself, complete with ruby-studded turban, to play host. All of these had been strictly forbidden to understand English except the Rajah himself, a former Oxford undergraduate.

The guests had been completely taken in; they had enjoyed the utter strangeness of their surroundings and the Atmosphere, with a capital A, lavishly provided for the usual stipend (plus certain extras). General de Lure, the *doyen* of the party, had been allowed secret access to the Rajah's armory. Here the Rajah

had demurred, resentful of this cheapening of his ancestral tro-
phies. The agency, anxious to satisfy so rich and faithful a client
as the General, had promised ample remuneration. Eventually,
since the General was a soldier and a nobleman, the Rajah had
generously consented to make an exception in his favor. Germain
had duly instructed the warriors and the dancing girls to take
part without protest, and with every appearance of piety, in the
prayer meetings and Bible readings organized on each trip by
Miss Angelica Simpson, a pillar of the New Baptist Church of
Burke City, South Dakota, U. S. A., and a redoubtable prose-
lytizer. The black slave, cowed by fifty years of captivity and
incidentally quite content with his lot, had been ordered to cling
like a faithful dog to the heels of Douglas Cadwallader IV of
Chicago, great-grandson of the General of that name who had
slaughtered so many Sioux and Apaches in the nineteenth century. Douglas, who was President of the Anti-Slavery League
of the Sons of the American Revolution, was preparing a monumental report to the United Nations on the aftereffects of slavery, and had already traveled for this purpose through Marti-
nique and Guadelupe, Guinea, Algeria and France, Gibraltar
and Macao. And so he had had a slave to himself. As for Liliane
Laage, Germain had originally considered letting her be ab-
ducted by a Sikh warrior, but had given up the plan for fear
the Sikh might go a little too far. Liliane Laage was herself a
constant source of adventures and it seemed wiser not to arrange
any more for her. However, the Sikh had played his part.

When the four travelers returned from Kashmir, and Germain
suggested Japan, they had immediately said yes and had studied
on the map the three islands with sibilant names: Kyushu, Shikoku, Honshu and the fourth island Hokkaido, farther north,
close to frozen Siberia. In their mind's eye they saw, too, a delicious maiden smiling welcome from under her parasol and
high-piled black coiffure. Liliane Laage declared that it was an
extraordinary country where you slept on the floor and ate raw
fish, where Judo champions floored their opponents with a few
words shouted in their ears. The American lady, Miss Simpson,

who always wanted to convert the whole world, had jumped at this opportunity of discovering a new heathen country. Gende Lure was interested in the Samurai and the heroes of the Pacific, Douglas Cadwallader in human welfare in the Far East. Two more tourists had joined the party: Nicole Marchard, whose father was treating her to a holiday abroad for her twenty-second birthday, and an Englishman in his forties, Cecil Brownley, notorious at the Agency for having once tried to bring back a Tahitian girl from the islands as housemaid. His letter of application had delighted the agency staff:

> DEAR GERMAIN,
>   You know my wife, and you won't be surprised to learn that I'm fed up with her. She reads the Bible aloud from morning till night and fills the house with gloomy clergymen. She's taken to calling me Brother Cecil, declares that she loves me in Christ, and when I tell her the pudding is burnt she replies that the ways of the Lord are mysterious. Be a good fellow and come to my rescue! I've just read somewhere that Japan is the only country in the world where women are lovely and, at the same time, obliging, gentle, obedient and not too hard to please. What heaven!
>
> Ever your sincerely,
CECIL BROWNLEY

Germain had said to himself that poor Cecil was on a wild-goose chase, but as it was in the Agency's interests . . .

He ran over in his mind the arrangements he had made: the Japanese inn, appropriately flimsy, with its dolls' house furniture, the marvelous garden where you felt lost after three steps, the surrounding peacefulness, broken only by the gong from the nearby temple, and all the pretty smiling maids at the inn waiting on you hand and foot, like gay, brightly-colored butterflies, whose mere presence took you out of this world, not to mention the indescribable Miyamoto, more Japanese than the Mikado himself, who looked so extremely solemn that you always wanted to laugh. . . .

Germain could set his mind at rest; everything would go off

all right, without exertion on his part. All he'd have to do, as usual, was to segregate his precious discoveries from the threatening sea of progress. It was a conjuring trick, but he believed in it. Throughout the world he hunted out the picturesque and the unusual, the exotic or the mysterious, detaching them carefully from their context, and thanks to this recipe the remotest regions of the earth were now dotted with ephemeral islets where the wealthy patrons of the Agency could be sent to indulge their fantasy. Thus in the past five years he had organized a number of voyages with increasing success: first had come "Visit to the Last Savages of the Congo," which had provided a witch doctor possessed by a devil, a fire dance, puberty rites, an attack on the camp by wild beasts, and the star attraction of the trip, of which he'd been so proud at the time—the rescuing helicopter which had dropped provisions to his party, although it was, in fact, already amply supplied. Then there had been "Gorilla Hunt," "Araucanian Mysteries," "On the Threshold of Red China" —actually Hong Kong, a perfectly peaceful town—and his last year's discovery, "Lost Island in the Pacific"—a harmless little island in Oceania where Germain's tourists had dismissed as mere mirages the radio station, dispensary and administrative offices, seen only the bamboo huts and scantily clad natives, and believed themselves genuine castaways. Finally, two months previously, "Adventure in Kashmir," with Cadwallader's slave, Liliane Laage's Sikh and Miss Simpson's converts so expertly conjured up. And today, following the same recipe, Japan, Land of the Rising Sun!

The same recipe? Was that quite true? Germain wondered. As usual, he had planned the setting, engaged the actors, seen to the local color and the requisite outlandishness. But for the first time in his career he had the impression that this fake was genuine, that this dream was the real thing, that the characters and the setting were authentic just because they were so cryptic, and that he was going to be caught in his own trap.

The telephone rang. He was informed from the office that a young woman wanted to speak to him.

34

"Who is she?" he asked.

"Miss Keiko Miyamoto. She says she'll only keep you five minutes."

Keiko Miyamoto? The little Jap's sister no doubt. Miyamoto had mentioned her briefly, assuring him that she would be a great help at the inn, since she spoke French and a little English. He had hired her sight unseen, for her brother's sake.

"All right, I'm coming down. Tell her to wait in the bar."

Keiko San went into the hotel bar and chose a seat in a quiet corner. She sat very straight, stiff and motionless, her legs pressed close together and tightly swathed in the plum-colored kimono, her prettiest kimono; she held her hands on her bag and her bag on her knees, and the obi formed a hard cushion between her back and the back of the chair. She kept her eyes cast down and half-closed between their dark lashes. The barman looked her over for a moment before taking her order. In her kimono, her white socks and lacquered wooden sandals, with her slender fingers innocent of nail polish and her face and lips discreetly made up, she did not look like a foreigner's tart. The barman disliked foreigners' tarts. All the Japanese disliked them, including the managers of the hotel, who notified their guests that Japanese women were not allowed in hotel bedrooms after 11 P.M. "American women? Certainly, sir, but no Japanese, absolutely forbidden by the management." The barman went up to her. Keiko San ordered some green tea.

She felt very frightened and was on the point of running away. She sipped her tea in an agony of indecision. Her brother would be furious if he found out what she had done. But she stayed on, longing to see the Frenchman appear and repeating to herself the introductory sentence she had prepared. For the past ten days her brother had been constantly telling her about Gilles Germain, his kindness, his easy manners, his anxiety to understand Japanese ways and the wonderful swiftness of his decisions. At first she paid little attention, then gradually she took an increasing interest until, one night, she awakened with a start, fancying she heard Germain speak to her. Romantic by nature like so many Japanese women, she had realized that morning that the unknown Frenchman was an important figure in her life, that she thought about him all day and waited impatiently for her brother's return to hear more about his words and actions. She had spent the whole of that day in thought and reverie, wondering whether this nascent feeling, which she dared scarcely admit even to herself, would bring shame on her family. A foreigner, here today and gone tomorrow! About five o'clock that afternoon she had set forth in search of Hato San the soothsayer, whose small table, lit by a single candle, was set up every day at that time in one of the main crossroads of the town. She had paid a considerable sum, three hundred yen, for a complete horoscope; she had her hand read and her face examined, and then asked for the test in which pieces of reed, divided into two bundles, foretell the future according to abstruse calculations known only to soothsayers. Hato San had spoken of a tall man who would bring her either happiness or unhappiness, he could not specify which. In any case, this was enough for her. Leaving the soothsayer she had jumped onto a streetcar, gone to the Marunuchi Hotel and bravely asked at the reception desk for M. Gilles Germain.

Brought up in the Japanese tradition to be passive and docile, the girl was unused to such daring and she waited there, more dead than alive, as the full extent of her rashness dawned on her. She remembered a girl friend of hers at the University, Akiko San, who had loved a foreign student. After two months of happiness he had gone off home, alone, without telling her, although he had promised to take her with him. For six long months Akiko had hoped for a letter or a message, then one evening she had taken her own life. Poor Akiko San! . . .

I'm crazy, utterly crazy, thought Keiko, and got up to go.

"You wanted to speak to me, mademoiselle?" said a voice close beside her.

The tall man was there, smiling at her. She bowed deeply and repeatedly. "Here we go again," Germain said to himself, and bowed back. He had acquired the art through much practice in his business dealings, but he had to bite his lips every time to stop himself from laughing.

"I am Miyamoto Keiko," she said, saying her surname first in the Japanese fashion.

"Your brother told me about you and I'm delighted to make your acquaintance."

He wondered how that ugly little man could have such an enchanting sister.

"Won't you have a drink with me?"

"Oh no, I must go home. My brother is waiting for me."

She raised her eyes furtively, then dropped them again, not daring to look him in the face. Germain noticed the whiteness of her skin and commented mentally, for the hundredth time, that this yellow race was not as yellow as one might have thought. In a whisper, she uttered the little sentence she had prepared: "My brother asks me to say . . . that he will be at . . . the airport . . . tonight."

"Thank you; please tell him I know I can depend on him."

She started bowing again, eager to be off. Then she left the bar with swift, tiny steps, gliding rather than walking over the carpet, a fragile and lovely porcelain figure come to life. Germain regretfully watched her disappear, puzzled as to why Mr. Miyamoto should have sent his sister to confirm once again what he had already confirmed by telephone an hour previously. After a few minutes' reflection he came to the conclusion, once again, that it was useless to ask oneself questions about the ways of the Japanese.

He dined alone in a nearby restaurant, and came back to the hotel bar to spend the few hours of peace left him before the arrival of the plane.

Cecil Brownley had made inquiries at Orly: "Yes, sir," the steward had told him, "we take on a Japanese hostess at Manila." And during the long flight from Paris, Brownley had savored the prospect of encountering his first specimen of so rare a race of women. His wife, indeed, had made a laudable effort during his last night in London, resignedly offering him her body. This happened two or three times a year, and Cecil always wondered if self-sacrifice was her motive, for he could see no other. He suspected her, during their brief moments of union, of begging the Lord's forgiveness for the outrage which she was forced to endure, and indeed of enduring it, on these few occasions, solely for the sublime pleasure of censuring herself and praying for her salvation. These rare deviations from saintliness were always followed by three months of exemplary living, largely occupied by devotions and good works. Having fulfilled his marital duties, Brownley had gone off with an easy conscience, leaving behind him a wife so burdened with shame that she could count on enjoying a long spell of penitence and prayer.

After the stop at Rome he had felt pleasantly drowsy. Airport girls are generally well worth looking at, but neither the dark-eyed Italians, the velvet-skinned Turks at Istanbul, the luscious Persian girls at Teheran nor the stately beauties of Karachi could win a single glance from him. Brownley was quite determined to be unfaithful to his wife, but not for one moment did he envisage disloyalty to the Japanese dream girl whom he had come to seek from the other side of the globe. When the plane stopped at Bangkok, however, the sight of a slender-necked Siamese girl roused him from his torpor; they were getting near. At Saigon he was ready, but the land hostess was a European. At last came Manila, where he waited with the rest of the party for the last stage of the journey and the reward of his long patience.

The loud-speaker shrilled: "Air France travelers for Toyko, please move over to the departure runway." The new aircraft was waiting; the hostess was Japanese. She waited smiling by the door of the plane, but not alone, for a French hostess stood by her side. Brownley compared the two, not without prejudice: the French girl's artificial smile, condescending air, chilly gaze and mannered pose, and the Japanese girl's naïve radiance, her grace, the blend of intensity and discretion in her glances and the lilt of her voice as she said, with a pretty bow, "Good evening, sir."

"Good evening, miss, I'm delighted to meet you."

She responded with a merry, spontaneous laugh. The French hostess, who was not laughing, hurried them in. The Japanese girl scored a great success as she offered chewing gum before the plane took off. Each of the passengers felt a flattering sense of receiving particular individual attention. General de Lure rose from his seat and bowed; Cadwallader gave an appreciative whistle; and Miss Simpson tried out the effect of traditional American heartiness on this young heathen with a "What's your first name? You must call me Angelica." Liliane Laage was amazed at the girl's grace and at the elegant cut of her blue suit: "Are you really Japanese?" Nicole Marchand alone reserved judgment; she was the best-looking and most intelligent member of the party. As for the Japanese hostess, she thought of nothing in particular, she merely offered chewing gum.

Brownley drifted into fantasy. A fleeting image of his wife emerged from a dark corner of his memory; he pushed it back, to relish undisturbed the first fruits of his future happiness. God bless the women of Japan!

But for all his intensive scrutiny of the hostess, he did not suspect that she was, in fact, a symbol of the modern Japanese girl. He was to meet her again everywhere, dressed in pale blue or white, red or navy, on every streetcar, train and bus, in the elevators and escalators of big stores, in restaurants—always indefatigably smiling, often armed with a microphone, announcing in her soft lilt the time the train would stop at the next station, the features of the landscape or the departments on each floor. For the modern girl is an essential cog in the vast machine of organized travel in Japan; it is she who shepherds those meek flocks of countryfolk, all beribboned with the same distinctive badge, to gape at the bustle and noise and dust of the city; who guides swarms of black-clad schoolboys and little girls in sailor suits through temples and pagodas; and who, on Sunday evenings, rounds up parties of excited urbanites, tipsy with sake, singing and reeling, after their day's outing in the country.

Later on, when finishing off his evenings with a round of the city's night clubs, Brownley was to meet her again among countless professionally charming hostesses, her uniform this time an excessively low-cut dance dress, excessively high-heeled shoes, artificial jewelry and short hair. Yet even here the modern girl displays the same spontaneous gaiety, smothering girlish laughter behind her fingers, dancing with unfailing zest, and eating an apple at her client's expense while he drinks alcohol. She'll go quite a bit of the way with you, at night, without resistance; money, you see, is hard to come by in Japan, and she takes it where she finds it, with the greatest of tact. . . .

A quarter of an hour after the plane had taken off, Liliane Laage suddenly noticed that the seat next to her was occupied by a legless cripple, yellow-skinned, sleeping with his mouth and eyes wide open. She uttered a shriek of terror. The cripple woke and gave her a glassy stare. She was in a state of collapse when the little hostess hurried up.

"Can I help you, madame? Aren't you feeling well?"

The cripple thrust out his legs, which had been folded under him, and got up to stretch himself.

"Oh, I beg your pardon . . . how very stupid of me," Liliane said to the hostess. "I . . . I thought this gentleman had no legs. I was frightened . . . he was sitting in such an odd position . . . please forgive me."

She was scarlet with shame. The hostess laughed heartily and explained that in Japan people preferred squatting on the floor, with their legs folded, to sitting in chairs, and that many Japanese, like this gentleman, were so used to this that the Western way of sitting gave them cramps. The pseudo-cripple asked some question in his own language. The hostess replied with a long sentence lasting five minutes, bowing twice during the course of it and four times at the end.

"Please make my apologies to this gentleman," Liliane said

in confusion. "I think this way of sitting is . . . er . . . simply marvelous, and so comfortable."

The hostess interpreted. The pseudo-cripple roared with laughter. Actually he was livid with resentment, but in Japan the greater one's embarrassment the louder one laughs. Encouraged by the general mirth Liliane tried to make amends for her blunder.

"In fact," she said, "I'm going to try it myself, since I'm to spend a whole month in your country."

She stood up on the chair, took off her shoes, and then knelt down. Three stitches in her stocking snapped, and two knee joints creaked.

"It's really delightful, and so graceful! Just like sitting on the grass! Am I doing it right? I do so want to live like a Japanese while I'm here. I'm so tired of modern comfort!"

She felt pins and needles in her right leg and shifted its position; her other stocking gave way. The pseudo-cripple, speechless with fury, was laughing himself sick. He had undeniably lost face! The hostess appreciated the poor man's anguish and realized how improper it was for a mere woman to witness such martyrdom; she fled to the cockpit until the victim had had time to resume his mask of dignity. At last he stopped laughing, sat down in the ordinary fashion and closed his eyes. Five more painful hours to endure till they reached Tokyo; then his torture would be at an end and his self-respect restored. For his one and only trip abroad had taught him that Japanese customs are not for export, and that if one wants to remain Japanese one must not stir from Japan. This woman by his side was bound to go flaunting her insolent ignorance of age-old practices through the country, unaware of her monstrous blunders.

He remembered one European couple whom he had often entertained for business reasons a few years previously. They had never stopped telling him: "You know, I eat raw fish now . . . I enjoy kneeling on the ground . . . I'm very good at making bows . . . I can sleep quite well on the mat," boasting as though of sensational feats, although ninety million Japanese derived their happiness and well-being from these actions. And he and his family had been obliged to laugh and congratulate them, saying how wonderful, how honored they were! When he'd had as much as he could stand he took to entertaining them only in Western-style restaurants and lodging them in luxury hotels with beds, asserting that all the Japanese inns were full. At this his guest went into fresh raptures: "So you can eat beefsteaks? you don't mind sleeping in beds? you shake hands?" He had assured them that he delighted in so doing, that he was going to build himself a Western-style house, that Japanese politeness was out of touch with modern life, all lies which he was forced to utter in order to save his guests, unawares, from loss of dignity. "Barbarians, the lot of them!" he said to himself, and on this comforting reflection he fell asleep.

When her neighbor had dozed off, Liliane Laage restored her legs to their normal position. "Lord, how ugly he is," she said to herself. "I hope they're not all like that!" She hoped it fervently, for the Sikh's embraces in Kashmir had given her a taste for Asia. Turning toward the porthole, she admired the fleecy carpet of clouds.

Miss Angelica Simpson's bony face was radiant with quiet bliss as she read over for the third time the letter from the minister of the New Baptist Church of Burke City, which had reached her the day before her departure.

DEAR SISTER:

I read your last letter at Sunday morning's meeting, knowing that your zeal for the Lord's truth would edify our brothers and sisters here in Burke City. We then recited with great fervor: *Who can find a virtuous woman? for her price is above rubies* (Proverbs xxxi, 10). Then, referring to the three neophytes whom, with God's help, you brought into the fold at Srinagar in faraway Kashmir, I spoke on the text: The heavens rejoice. Your story of the conversion of the Rajah's dancers, who laid down their amulets before you in token of their rejection of false gods, brought tears to the eyes of our sisters. I understand your distress at having to leave your three converts unguided in the midst of a country sunk in ignorance and sin. A friend of mine, a young minister, is willing to go out to Srinagar to set up a permanent mission there. We have drafted an estimate for our settlement there: seven thousand dollars for the first year. I allotted Sunday's collection to this end: fifty-nine dollars thirty cents. I should be glad if you would let me have your opinion about this mission. With best wishes for your journey from our brethren and sisters and from myself.

Sincerely,
DAVID WOLF

"That man's certainly an angel from heaven," she said aloud.

Cecil Brownley, who was in the next seat, reading, gave a start.

"I beg your pardon, were you speaking to me, Miss Simpson?"

"Oh, pardon me, I was thinking out loud—it's a habit of mine when I've something important on my mind. I was thinking of David, our minister. I must write him before we land."

Brownley groaned. He had not been in the Srinagar party and was unacquainted with Miss Simpson's pious eccentricities. He had a mental picture of the grim-faced clergy who called on his wife.

"A minister—good heavens! Of what denomination?"

"New Baptists. I'm in charge of missions to Asiatic countries."

"So that's why you're going to Japan?" (He could not believe his ears; a strict Baptist in the land of geishas! A woman to be avoided at all costs.) "How very interesting, Miss Simpson. I'll leave you to your writing."

He had no wish for further acquaintance.

Angelica sent for a tray and laid it on her knees, pulled from the thick leather brief case which went everywhere with her a sheet of pink writing paper headed: *New Baptist Church of Burke City, South Dakota,* unscrewed her fountain pen, reflected for a few moments and then wrote:

DEAR BROTHER:

Many thanks for your most welcome letter. I have written my

bank to transmit to you as soon as possible a first check for five thousand dollars. I hope your friend will be able to go out very soon. I am chiefly worried about our brother in Kashmir. His piety is most edifying, but a Catholic mission, a Lutheran mission, an Anglican one and, I believe, a Christian Science preacher have already laid siege to his soul. So true are the words of the prophet Jeremiah: *Trust ye not in lying words, saying, The temple of the Lord, the temple of the Lord, the temple of the Lord, are these.* (Jer.vii.4) He ought to be given teaching quickly, and better teaching than I could provide in so short a time. Our two sisters seem to me to be more firmly rooted in the true faith, but there is a further problem in their case: they must renounce their profession without delay. Much as they abominate their worldly calling, it ensures their daily bread. Were they decently clad, they might doubtless be of great service to their new minister. As for myself, dear brother, I am preparing to land in Japan in three hours' time: ninety million heathen and idolators! As in all the crucial moments of my life, I open my Bible to find there strength and courage . . .

Angelica pulled a pocket Bible out of her brief case, opened it and read aloud: "Confounded be all they that serve graven images, that boast themselves of idols: worship him, all ye gods."

Cecil Brownley stared at her in amazement. Remembering his wife, he instinctively replied "Amen!" Angelica threw him a grateful glance, copied out the Psalm and went on with her letter.

Never have I invoked the word of the Lord in vain, brother. My first meeting with a member of the Japanese people promises well. A simple, openhearted girl who made no bones about admitting that she practiced two religions: Shinto and Buddhism. I questioned why she had chosen these faiths, to which she replied: "Because my father did so." I rejoiced to hear this explanation, since a creed which is acquired, one might almost say imposed by mere family tradition, cannot long withstand the challenge of the true faith. My own mother was a Mormon, my father a Methodist, while yours I think were Presbyterians, and see how the Holy

Truth fills us both with strength and light. My hopes are high. I will keep you informed.

Sincerely,
ANGELICA SIMPSON

"O Lord, help Thy humble servant . . ." She fell asleep, worn out by her fervor.

Douglas Cadwallader IV, President of the Anti-Slavery League of the Sons of the American Revolution, was deep in thought. Japan was a complex problem. According to all his information, slavery assumed such subtle forms there that proof of it might be hard to come by. No blatant bondage such as he had seen in Kashmir, for instance, one of the finest cases he had dealt with during his travels: that black slave of the Rajah's who, under his skillful persuasion, had confided such a piteous story. Poor man, what would have become of him had not Fate brought Douglas Cadwallader IV across his path? The thought of it still stirred him; he recalled the Negro's touching farewell at the gates of the palace which had been his prison. A strange story indeed! The Rajah, ignorant of the extent of his wealth and the number of his servants, was unaware of the existence of this man, a forgotten legacy from his father, who had ruled in the bygone days of the British Raj. He had raised no sort of objection to selling the slave to Cadwallader, declaring indeed that he would gladly have made a present of him, but for the necessity of handing down the family patrimony intact to his son. Cadwallader had freed the Negro on the spot and provided him with a certificate of emancipation, duly signed by his late owner. *Life* had published a photostat of the document, together with a letter of congratulation from Pandit Nehru attributing this deplorable anachronism to the shocking customs inherited from Pakistani tradition. . . . But what about Japan? He would surely not find slavery there in its classic form, although experience had taught him that outside America you could never be certain; Africa and Asia must *a priori* be considered as still po-

45

tent hotbeds of *de facto* slavery, and Japan, which had only emerged during the last hundred yers from military feudalism, could be no tbetter than the rest.

"But be careful," a high official of the State Department had exhorted him, "be very careful! Japan is our most loyal ally in the Pacific, a vital factor in the defense of the United States in that part of the world, and you must on no account imperil the traditional friendship between our two countries by some rash move. Why don't you go to French Sahara? You'll find material enough there to carry out your mission, and a very useful mission it would be, believe me."

Cadwallader preferred Japan, which was indispensable for the completion of his report.

"In that case," continued the diplomat, "I can only give you two pieces of advice. First, read this pamphlet which we have been distributing to all American soldiers stationed in Japan since the Peace Treaty was signed: *Japan, Our Friend and Ally.* Next, you should concentrate on the question of geisha girls and prostitutes. You know there are about five hundred thousand of these in Japan. They're practically a piece of folklore, which alters neither the painful urgency of the problem nor their servile status. But they do attract tourists, and the Japanese government condones a certain amount of publicity about them. You can draw attention to this without damage to our policy. But please don't go any further. We all know, in the Department, that the condition of the working class, particularly of the women, in Japan is no better than slavery in disguise, that the old code of honor and loyalty keeps the mass of the people in an intolerable state of moral bondage, that the rights of women are acknowledged in the Constitution but not by the peasantry —we know all that but we never speak about it."

Tokyo in an hour's time! Cadwallader felt strangely excited. Those geishas, bought like cattle and subject to the most hateful coercion. He would fly to their aid! From the depths of their prisons they appealed to him.

46

Nicole Marchand was reading. Why think about Japan, why form preconceived notions of a country she did not know? Unlike her traveling companions she had seen no point in studying the subject beforehand; she wanted to start off with open eyes and an unprejudiced mind.

General de Lure had been asleep ever since Manila. On the eve of battle he always slept soundly. In his time this precious gift had brought him fame among his fellow soldiers. It was supposed to betoken lucid calm and great strength of character, although people whispered respectfully that it was more or less a matter of habit. Before dropping off he would tell his subordinate officers: "I have done what's necessary, God will do the rest." An unfriendly deity had brought about his premature retirement in 1940. Having written his memoirs (*France Has Saved The World: an Eyewitness Account*) he was now devoting the rest of his life to traveling the globe. At the predetermined hour, he awoke fit and fresh, and consulted his watch: 11:40. Outside the plane it was night.

"We land in twenty minutes," he told Nicole, his neighbor. "You're young and you've probably not traveled much yet. How wonderful for you to think that in a few minutes you'll be in Japan."

"To tell you the truth, General, I couldn't care less. People make far too much fuss about the place."

The voice of the hostess announced through the loud-speaker: "We shall shortly be landing at Tokyo; kindly fasten your safety belts and do not smoke. Thank you." There followed a long tirade in Japanese.

"That must be the translation of what we've just been told in French," said the general. "Did you notice that it takes four times as long in Japanese?"

He had unwittingly hit on the key to Japan.

Mr. Miyamoto uttered a long-drawn-out moan of delight. From the wooden tub only his head emerged, streaming with

47

sweat and surrounded by a thick cloud of steam. The rest of his naked body was simmering at a temperature of 105 degrees. Sitting in the tub with his knees drawn up to his chin, he reveled in the delights of the *o furo*. He thrust his arm out of the water, seized a china cup and a flask of sake standing on a shelf, and drank with his eyes shut. Such had been the custom of his father the General when taking his daily bath; outside, the orderly would be waiting with his horse, holding its bridle in one hand and a flask of sake in the other. The General, fresh and clean, would go out into the porch, toss off his sake, mount his horse and ride off to the barracks. He had been a real man, the General, he had known how to live! Horses were out of date and so were soldiers, the General had died a Japanese patriot's death, but that evening Mr. Miyamoto was going to revive the family tradition. His modern mount—a comfortable Chevrolet taxi, picked out a little while before from a score of others at the best taxi stand in the district—would call for him presently at his own front door and drive him to the airport. He got out of the bath and proceeded to wring out his towel, which was soaked; Mr. Miyamoto had taken it into the bath with him, according to the Japanese custom which requires you to wash yourself before the bath with a dry towel and to dry yourself afterwards with the same towel, wet. Finished, he slipped on an indoor kimono and went into his bedroom. He felt his mind alert, as all Japanese do on emerging from the *o furo*. Finding he still had an hour to spare before the taxi was due, he knelt down at his table and picked up a book which was lying there. Seizing a piece of paper already covered with lists of words like *sincèrement, souvent, précocement, modestement* and so forth, he resumed his steady hunt for adverbs through the work of George Sand. He worked swiftly, without wasting time over the meaning of the text. The only thing that mattered was to count and classify the adverbs used by the French authoress and to publish the results of this research. Mr. Miyamoto was convinced of the vital importance of such an undertaking for the study of the French language. He had spoken of it to the director of the French School in

Tokyo, who had said "So what?" clearly implying, by this laconic retort, his keen interest in the project.

Having filled a whole page with columns of adverbs he closed the book. Now he changed his kimono for Western dress; in the pocket of his jacket he found Gilles Germain's last letter. He re-read it with deep delight.

> Dear Mr. Miyamoto:
>
> I should like first of all to express my thanks for your extreme obligingness and your invaluable help in the organization of my tourists' visit. I can assure you in all sincerity that I could not possibly have accomplished so arduous a task without your assistance, and I trust that I may count on your intelligent and efficient assistance in the days ahead of us. [Germain obviously understood the Japanese mentality.] May I remind you that you are to be solely responsible for meeting the party on April 2nd, since I am anxious that their introduction to Japan should be made under the exclusive guidance of a Japanese. I shall however be available at the inn between one and three in the morning in the unlikely case of your needing my assistance. In the meantime, dear Mr. Miyamoto, pray accept the assurance of my very sincere good wishes and my profoundest gratitude.

The last phrase had particularly delighted Mr. Miyamoto. He did not quite know what it meant, but sensed in it a subtlety worthy of the traditions of the great French nation. He uttered it aloud: "Pray accept the assurance . . ." There are only two civilized countries in the world, he said to himself, France and Japan. He knelt before a mirror and repeated slowly, with a gracious smile to his own reflection: "Pray accept the assurance of my very sincere good wishes and my profoundest gratitude." What a lovely sentence! he thought.

The hooting of a motor horn interrupted his declamation. He rushed out, and saw the chauffeur standing by the front doorstep. Putting on his sternest expression, Mr. Miyamoto seized a bottle of sake and drank it all before the astonished eyes of the chauffeur. The late General Miyamoto, of the Army of the Rising Sun, might have been proud of his son. He slipped on his shoes

49

and walked with great dignity toward the car. The chauffeur bowed to a ninety degree angle and opened the door of the taxi.

"Haneda Airport," said Mr. Miyamoto curtly. Then he lapsed into silence.

On the roof of the main building of Haneda Airport there stands a small Shinto temple painted vermilion, dedicated to the spirits of the place, which guarantees safe landings. The Air-France plane from Paris therefore landed at midnight without accident and drew up on the runway. Having passed rapidly through the hands of considerate customs officers, the six tourists from the Unknown Lands Travel Agency gathered in the main hall: Liliane Laage, Angelica Simpson, Nicole Marchand, Cecil Brownley, Douglas Cadwallader IV, and General de Lure. They were looking around for Germain's familiar figure when a dapper little Japanese came up to them, a broad smile illuminating his flat face.

"On behalf of Monsieur Germain, who has asked me to make his apologies, and on my own behalf, I welcome you to Japan; pray accept the assurance of my sincerest good wishes and my profoundest gratitude."

They were dumfounded. Quite imperturbably the little man turned to General de Lure, the oldest of the men in the party, and held out his visiting card. He moved in a curious way, bent forward as if he had been sitting down for too long.

"May I introduce myself," he said. "I am Mr. Miyamoto, Assistant to the Director of the Unknown Lands Agency."

General de Lure was preparing to reply when his interlocutor suddenly vanished from his field of vision, doubled over in an impeccable Japanese bow. The general followed suit awkwardly; he was a proud and honorable man who had never bowed to anyone. Little Miyamoto remained doubled over; it would have been highly improper for him to have stood upright first. The general, exceedingly embarrassed, ducked even lower, hoping to wear out Miyamoto. But the latter, his head slightly on one side, was watching out of the corner of his eye for the general to draw himself up again, so that he could promptly synchronize his own upward movement and stand upright neither before his bowing partner, which would imply that he was superior to him, nor after, which would betoken too great a degree of inferiority. In order to avoid mistakes either way it is customary to rise by stages, as a frogman ascends from the deep, pausing first at an angle of sixty degrees, then at one of forty-five and finally at one of thirty. Alas the general, unfamiliar with this procedure, drew himself up all at once, and only Mr. Miyamoto's extreme agility enabled him to reach a vertical position at the same moment. He would never have forgiven himself otherwise. The same ceremony was repeated with the other two gentlemen of the party, the women being entitled only to an abbreviated version of it with less sweeping bows.

At the open door of the Air-France coach a brief verbal scuffle ensued between General de Lure and Mr. Miyamoto, the Frenchman seeking to make way for the three ladies and the Japanese insistently urging the men to climb in first.

"What does it matter," said Nicole, "we can go in by different doors."

Mr. Miyamoto glared at her, instinctively recognizing an adversary. At last the visitors and their luggage were settled in and the coach drove off, headlights ablaze, through the darkness of Toyko.

Germain took a taxi to a rural suburb an hour and a half from the city center. Having delegated the invaluable Miyamoto with his smiles and bows to give a proper Japanese welcome to the six tourists, thus plunging them into an unfamiliar atmosphere, he was going to keep out of the way and leave them to tackle the *japonaiseries* he had prepared for them. After a dozen halts to allow the chauffeur to ask the way—the streets of Tokyo are not named and the houses not numbered—the taxi deposited him beside a large, typically Japanese villa surrounded by a garden; this was the luxurious inn he had chosen for his tourists' residence. He motioned the driver to wait a little farther off, and looked at his watch: one A.M. They would soon be here. He concealed himself behind a bank and waited.

On either side of the small doorway, hanging from the tiled porch roof that was shaped like a circumflex accent, two lanterns were gleaming, one red and the other white, inscribed with a Chinese character like a gigantic spider. In the garden, the foliage of the bamboos swayed gently in the night breeze. Behind the paper *shoji* over the lighted windows, women's shadows passed to and fro. Laughter could be heard; Japanese maids were always laughing as they went about their work. Fugitive gleams, like reflected lights in a mirror, flickered here and there round the house. Pieces of silver paper hung on the eaves caught the moonlight as they twisted and turned in the wind. Tiny bells were hung among them and tinkled at the least puff of air, their clear yet timid note enhancing the freshness of the garden. Farther off to the right rose the silent mass of a Buddhist temple, its façade patterned with the black silhouettes of two twisted pines. To the left were two wooden summerhouses with curving roofs, surrounded by a fence. And in the far distance lay the great city, Tokyo. Light footsteps sounded on the gravel path, and Keiko San, lovely Keiko San, appeared, framed in the doorway. A small tilted nose, two enormous slanting eyes, pale skin, gleaming black hair, a plum-colored kimono, girlish gestures; Germain stared at her as if he'd never seen her before. Keiko San took a few steps along the path, watching for the sound of the car which would bring the strangers. Germain climbed up onto his bank.

"Keiko San . . . Keiko San," he called softly.

She stopped and recognized him.

"Good evening, Monsieur Germain," she said with a smile.

Her voice was as soft as the little bells in the garden. Something strange happened then; his feelings for this girl, whom he had thought of as an easy conquest, changed in the space of an instant to adoration. Japan is like that, disappointing, drab and dull, and then suddenly, like a fleeting vision, comes an image of perfection—a corner in a garden, a stone lantern, a half-open window, an attitude, a girl's figure, glimpses of inimitable grace —and you cannot help but respond. He moved toward her. She had not stirred. They stood motionless for a moment. She looked him in the eyes now; in her own setting she was not afraid. Germain took her by the shoulders, with gentle care, as one takes up a precious picture.

"Keiko San . . . I love you."

He could not have said otherwise. He had spoken on an impulse. He might take back his words tomorrow, but at that moment any man would have uttered them. He kissed her softly on the forehead and nose and then on the lips.

"Gilles San," she said in Japanese, "you are like a clear stream on a spring morning."

He did not understand the words, but he knew they meant I love you. For the Japanese don't say I love you, they use roundabout poetic phrases instead, pretty comparisons which attain their end quite as surely as lovers' words.

Then she raised her hand to her mouth, slipped from his embrace and ran back to the house. "I'm behaving like a boy of fifteen this evening," he said to himself, "I'm insane . . ." She passed through the open door and the paper lantern spotlighted her figure with a rosy glow.

It's a stage setting, thought Germain as he watched the scene, but somehow it's completely natural and true and harmonious, without one false note. He had had no difficulty in finding this house; there were only too many to choose from. There are thousands of equally attractive places surrounding Tokyo. Most foreigners, wedded to their Grand Palaces and their sirloin steaks, never discover them.

The scene grew lively behind the lighted *shoji* of the villa. Keiko San, back in the inn, spoke a few words; he recognized the silvery tone of her voice. Other voices, gay and high-pitched, answered her. The actors were ready, the stage was set, the prompter in his place behind the bank. The curtain could now go up.

III

At the Pine Wind Inn

———

After an hour and a half's dreary journeying through unlighted streets—Tokyo, apart from its fluorescent street signs, is one of the worst-lit capitals in the world—the car turned into a narrow lane and slowed down. The general remarked to Miyamoto: "*Mon fils,* one can't see a thing in your country! If I didn't trust you implicitly, I should suspect foul play. Have we much farther to go?"

The little man protested inwardly: the honorable general might at least have called him Mr. Miyamoto!

"Only a few minutes more . . ."

He considered his personal problem and decided that by mentioning his father, that glorious soldier, he would win unfailing respect. He quickly worked out a suitable transition and announced: "We are due to reach your residence at a quarter to two, that's to say in five minutes. I think we shall be there on time, for my father brought me up in the army tradition of punctuality, and I am anxious not to fail in that respect so early in our acquaintance."

"Oh, your father was an officer?" asked the general.

"A general, monsieur!"

A voice remarked from the depths of the car: "We sure knocked the hell out of them!" Cadwallader was offering his opinion with simple American forthrightness.

"Wonderful soldiers," said the general tactfully. "Best infantry in the world, outside France and Germany. I'd be happy to meet your father, we could compare our experiences."

Mr. Miyamoto began to chuckle, then to laugh outright.

"What's so funny about what I said?" puzzled the general.

"He's dead," tittered the Japanese.

This piece of information accompanied by so strange a display of merriment, fell like an icy cloak over the six occupants of the car. Brownley coughed, and the general mumbled, "Oh, I beg your pardon!"

"There can't have been much love lost between them," murmured Nicole.

"Did he die in the war?" inquired Cadwallader.

"In the Kuril Islands in 1945."

"But we hadn't landed there then," said the American, surprised.

"My honorable father died by his own hand, according to the rites, on August 15th at 10 A.M. with all his staff."

Speechless with amazement, the six travelers heard this terrible story recounted as an uproariously funny joke.

"The previous day," Mr. Miyamoto went on, "His Majesty the Emperor Showa, heartbroken at the thought of his people's sufferings, had decided to break off a hopeless battle. The news of the decision reached my father by radio on the island where he was in command. He had not been defeated, in fact he had repelled all the American advances, but the August Voice had spoken. He made his decision quickly, as befitted a son of the Samurai." (Here Mr. Miyamoto practically choked with suppressed laughter.) "Bowing toward the Imperial Palace, he thrust his sword into his bowels, ha ha! and the Chief of Staff, his best friend, cut off his head at one blow, ha ha ha! Then the Chief of Staff himself committed hara-kiri, and his head was cut off by a colonel. After the colonel came a major, then all the

56

officers in turn down to the last lieutenant. The latter, having nobody left to behead him, tried unsuccessfully to blow himself up with a grenade. He brought home the ashes of his superior officers, and it was he who told me of my father's glorious death, ha ha ha!"

Mr. Miyamoto seemed delighted with his tale. Liliane, picturing that horrible succession of severed heads, moaned softly to herself, "What men!" Nicole shut her eyes and a shudder ran through her, but to her this mass suicide seemed merely stupid, and she quite failed to appreciate its romantic and quixotic grandeur. General de Lure consoled himself with the thought that he had belonged to a sensible army where such barbaric practices were not in use. Suppose he had had to disembowel himself in company with General Gamelin and hundreds of others? Appalling thought! Collecting himself, he passed silent censure on the suicide's son. How shocking to hear a young man laugh at the account of his father's noble sacrifice! The new generation, of course! Unfortunate Japan, your glorious traditions are finished when your sons make fun of them. He was grieved about it, feeling nonetheless that this spectacular heroism shed a certain glory on the entire military profession which had lost some of its prestige since swords went out.

But the general was mistaken; Mr. Miyamoto had a vast respect for his father, and if he laughed, it was because a well-brought-up Japanese is bound by habit to laugh at any painful or pathetic subject, so that his hearers may not be embarrassed or distressed by a tale of misfortunes that do not concern them. The result, however, was quite the opposite. An insurmountable discomfort possessed the party, since nobody but a Nipponese is capable of appreciating such a refinement of sensibility. The general decided that the term, *mon fils,* by which he was wont to address young men whose looks he liked, could no longer be used to this unnatural son.

"Mr. Miyamoto," he said, stressing the Mr., "I'm sure all present join with me in expressing deepest sympathy."

The little Japanese was thrilled: He said *Mr.* Miyamoto!

Wonderful people, these French! How quickly they understand!

The car stopped at last in front of a small wooden gate, lit up as though for a street fair. They climbed out. The driver honked loudly; in the garden, colored lights suddenly shone amid the foliage, red and blue, green and white, gleaming rainbowlike in the darkness. Smiling girls came tripping up, hobbled by their long kimonos of white and green, red and blue. With their arms hanging straight and their elbows close to their sides, they bowed prettily together. Mr. Miyamoto, like the leading man in the closing scene of a revue surrounded by a bevy of dancers, bowed too, and said, "Allow me to welcome the honorable visitors to their modest home, Matsukaze, the Wind in the Pines. Kindly deign to enter!"

The reception committee seized the luggage and went skipping past the honorable visitors, who were completely spellbound. Here at last was the Japan they had longed for, the picture-book Japan, a paradise of loveliness such as every man dreams of in secret. Little Miyamoto, that frog-faced cynic, seemed a fairy-tale magician. With one wave of his hand he had conjured lanterns and flowers and fair women up out of the night. He led his guests by a roundabout path, the prettiest in the whole garden, thickly carpeted with dark green moss, with flat steppingstones at regular intervals.

"Moss is the most precious ornament in our Japanese gardens," Mr. Miyamoto intoned. "Would you be so very obliging as to keep to the stones."

So, hopping from one stone to the next, in single file, the party reached the house, admiring on their way the quiet little pool in which broad lotus leaves were floating. The door of the villa, one step up, opened on a large bare low-ceilinged room with walls of ivory parchment framed by brown wooden posts. The girls were here again, and now there were more of them. Brownley counted six, kneeling side by side, and found them all attractive. Miyamoto performed the necessary introductions, and an elderly woman in a gray kimono started off the inevitable series of bows.

"Madame Hashi, the manager," he said. "She is highly honored to receive you here and she feels certain that your presence will bring her house seven years of happiness."

The lady, who had not yet opened her mouth, uttered a few words in Japanese.

"Madame Hashi," Miyamoto went on quite unperturbed, "has just made the remark which I translated for you."

Nicole Marchand made a mental note to be suspicious of Miyamoto's translations in the future. But their guide proceeded: "Keiko San, my sister. She speaks French."

The plum-colored kimono bowed. "Please, tank you welly much," she said.

The guests bowed awkwardly to Mme. Hashi, and then to Keiko San.

"These girls are the maids of the inn. One of them will be waiting on each of you."

Everybody bowed to the maids, who bowed back, and were bowed to again, and so forth. In this bowing contest the Japanese team won easily, being in better training.

At the doorstep the visitors took off their shoes and put on slippers, then were led separately, each by a maid, to their respective bedrooms. Brownley was disappointed to see the plum-colored kimono disappear with Liliane Laage. A girl in a white kimono with blue flowers and blue obi had been allotted to him; she had a broad flat face, healthy and apple-cheeked, sturdy hips, and round forearms which emerged prettily from the huge sleeves of her kimono.

The sliding doors closed and each visitor found himself standing on a mat, in socks or stockings, in a paper room, alone with a smiling Japanese girl. Two minutes had gone by when wild shrieks rang out from Miss Simpson's room. Miyamoto, who was on guard at the junction of the corridors, dashed up as Angelica's horrified face peered out through the half-open door.

"Shocking! It's shocking! I don't know what's possessed this girl, she insists on trying to undress me! Tell her to go away, I can't make her understand a thing."

59

"It is the custom, Miss Simpson," Miyamoto replied. "But of course if you would rather . . ."

Angelica thought for a moment. Her proselytizing project involved fraternization and respect for the customs of others.

"All right . . . But ask her at least to turn toward the wall while I undress."

Meanwhile all the guests in their various bedrooms were experiencing that amazement which is the invariable Western reaction to the extreme attentiveness of Japanese chambermaids. The role of these girls, taken for granted in all inns with any pretensions to luxury, is to undress you, to wrap you in a special-colored kimono, to scrub you in the bath, to kneel beside you during the whole of your meal, to tuck you in between the *futons* (quilts which serve both as mattress and covering, spread on the floor), and to wait until you are asleep to wish you good night and put out the light.

The general had been through worse ordeals during his military career. Thus everything went smoothly for him from the start. The maid pointed imperatively to a brown kimono lying folded on the mat, so he took off his jacket, waistcoat and tie, and waited. Then she came close and pointed to his shirt, saying *dozo* (please) in such a pretty, coaxing voice that he unfastened his collar and cuffs with a smile. She took the shirt, and gave a sudden squeal of delight as she ran her slender fingers through the gray hair that covered his chest. The Japanese are hairless, and she gazed at this curly fleece with the naïve rapture of a child discovering a new toy. The general patted her cheek with a fatherly air and held out his arms for his kimono. *"Dozo,"* said the maid, pointing to his trousers. Somewhat reluctantly now the general turned away and unfastened his belt. The girl came and stood in front of him. He turned away again; she followed him around. So for the sake of peace and quiet, he pulled off his trousers. She folded them carefully and burst into laughter as she pointed to his shorts.

"Oh no," said the general, "that's going a bit far!"

He wore the kind of short trunks found throughout the Occidental world. The girl, however, had never seen a man thus clad, for the Japanese use long, clinging cotton tights, which are very comfortable in their unheated houses. She laughed louder than ever; there was something so comical about this hairy-chested man in a woman's panties! Standing barefoot on the mat, shamefaced as a raw recruit in front of this brazen young woman, the general lost his temper.

"Kimono," he ordered. "Kimono!"

She handed it to him and he swiftly slipped it on. As he did so, she moved close to him and put both arms around him to fasten the sash. He felt her bosom against his stomach, for she was quite tiny, and he suddenly remembered that he was only sixty.

Liliane Laage stripped quickly, without argument. She despised false modesty. Keiko San marveled at her black lingerie and the lace on her petticoat. Liliane at forty was still a very handsome woman, slim-waisted, round-hipped, firm-breasted. Keiko San noticed this, and passed an admiring hand over the shapely white body. Being small-bosomed herself like most Japanese, she lingered in exploration of the Frenchwoman's breasts. Liliane, startled, stared at her in amazement. She had had no such experience before, but why not? . . . Keiko San was smiling. Liliane felt herself blush, and, all her senses alert, allowed the kimono to be slipped on and the sash tied. Having accomplished her duties, the girl bowed and left the room.

Mr. Miyamoto escaped from the corridor and went outside. He found Germain pacing up and down in the darkness.

"Everything is satisfactory," he told him. "They all seem quite happy, except for the honorable American lady who refuses to let the maid help her. I'm sorry about that, for Mme. Hashi will scold the poor girl."

"Don't worry," Germain reassured him. "I know her quite well, she'll end by submitting like everybody else. In any case, remember that our clients want to be treated like Japanese. They've paid a good price for that sole purpose. You mustn't make any concessions to them, for they won't be at all grateful."

61

"Even about the bath?" asked Miyamoto, aware of American prudery.

"Even about the bath . . ." He paused for a moment in thought. "But who is your sister with?"

"With Mme. Laage. I'd rather . . ."

"Perfect"—he had come to consider Keiko San as his private property—"perfect! Since things are going so well, I'll be off. I'll call you tomorrow evening. Good night."

He got into his taxi and went off to his Western-style bed in the Marunuchi Hotel.

In the corridor, Mr. Miyamoto met Mme. Hashi in a great state of agitation.

"The honorable *furo* is ready," she said.

He broadcast the news among his guests, but only the Englishman and the French girl favored a bath at the late hour. Mme. Hashi displayed shocked surprise. She ran through the rooms, bursting in unceremoniously and calling out in threatening tones: "*O furo dozo! O furo dozo!*" Cadwallader yelled to her, "You might knock first!" which was a waste of time, for the staff of Japanese inns wander about everywhere with the utmost freedom.

Cecil Brownley, comfortably wrapped in his brown kimono and prepared to try every experiment, followed Mme. Hashi. Tomoko San, his personal attendant in the white kimono, brought up the rear. All three stopped before a sliding door of frosted glass. Mme. Hashi opened it, showed them into a tiny room, bowed and withdrew discreetly, closing the door. Brownley, alone with Tomoko San, took off his kimono and his trunks, which she folded and laid in a basket. He was beginning to get used to walking about naked in her company. The girl opened another door and beckoned to him. At first he could make out nothing in the steam-laden atmosphere, but he stepped forward cautiously over the damp, slippery tiled floor, while the girl guided him by the hand. Then, in the middle of the room he saw a giant kidney-shaped tub edged with green mosaic, as big as a swimming pool. The water appeared scalding hot; clouds of steam were rising so that the end of the huge room was lost in mist. Tomoko San made him sit down on a small low stool, filled a pail with hot water and poured it over his body. Then she soaped him thoroughly from head to foot. Brownley began to feel embarrassed. He had nothing within reach, no bathrobe, no towel. And the girl was vigorously soaping his stomach. At last she stopped and prepared to rinse him. Then she pointed to the *o furo;* and, offered an escape from the situation, he plunged into it, not without a muffled yell, for the water was extremely hot. Tomoko San disappeared and Brownley breathed again. The bath was enjoyable, you could almost swim in it. He lolled at ease until he heard the noise of the sliding doors again. Two people came into the room, invisible through the thick vapor that rose from the bath. There was a prolonged sound of rubbing. Somebody being washed, he thought. The stranger got into the bath and then called out, "Oh, it's hot!" Through the steam he made out what was undeniably a female figure: it was Nicole. He felt her tread on his foot.

"Why, there's somebody in this bath!" she said, and ducked into the water up to her neck.

"I'm terribly sorry, mademoiselle, I confess I'm as surprised as you are . . ."

He could not think what else to say.

"I never imagined there would be mixed bathing here. Anyhow I made sure I was alone, there were no clothes in the anteroom. I must have come in by a different door."

They looked at one another with embarrassment, only their heads sticking up from the water. Then Nicole abruptly burst into laughter.

"Really, we must look too stupid! However, as much as I enjoy your company, I must ask you to look the other way while I get out of here."

He did so, then climbed out himself to be promptly pounced on by Tomoko San, his white-robed attendant. She dried him, then proceeded to give him a rubdown, pummelling his shoulder blades with her fists. . . .

63

All the visitors gathered for supper, kneeling round a big low table and dressed as Japanese. The six maids were there too, each devoting smiles and attentions exclusively to her particular client. Mr. Miyamoto briefly demonstrated the use of chopsticks, and everybody tried them, with varying success. Tomoko San came to Brownley's aid, taking his hands in her own to guide them; he quite enjoyed this little game. The table was crammed with dozens of small bowls, cups, saucers, square plates, rectangular plates, oval plates, all of pretty china or lacquer. Was it a dinner? Each dish held but a mouthful. Herbs, stalks, seaweed, brown sauce, salted cabbage, some white tremulous substance that looked like cream cheese but wasn't, various unidentifiable gelatinous compounds presumably derived from deep-sea fish, octopus tentacles cut in rounds and monstrous shell-less crustaceans, all served cold, not to mention small squares of red meat which Liliane Laage recognized as raw tuna fish.

They ate a hearty supper and went to bed delighted at being Japanese. . . .

The *shoji* over her windows were barely showing daylight when Angelica awoke. She groped about over the mat in search of her watch. A quarter to six. She had slept little and badly, stifled by the *futon*. She felt feverish. Feverish? Impossible. Miss Simpson's iron constitution was famous in her home town. It was probably just the excitement of finding herself stretched out on a straw mat on the floor of a paper house. As she slid her other hand from under the covers she touched her own skin. Oh, she thought, have I been sleeping naked? Such a misfortune had not happened to her in forty-eight years. Her *yucata*, a flimsy night-kimono, had worked itself up during the night and was twisted round her neck. She wriggled until she had restored herself to a more decent condition. Then she emerged from her covers and opened a *shoji*.

Day had dawned and the sun was shining on the still surface of the garden pool, where a stone lantern stood gazing at its reflection. Angelica liked walking in the early morning, when God seemed nearer and somehow less terrible. She looked around for her clothes. The room was bare and amazingly tidy—the bed-covers in the middle, with a low lamp, a carafe and glass, a minute dressing table in one corner, a stove with dead cinders and nothing else. No skirt, no sweater, no stockings or petticoat; her bags and cases had vanished too. She remembered that a smiling girl in a kimono had put everything away before dinner. But where? The room was surrounded by sliding doors painted a pretty ivory white. She investigated. The doors on the far wall opened onto the passage, those on the right. . . . Probably a cupboard, she thought. She opened them: there, half covered by a red-and-white flowered *futon*, lay General de Lure sound asleep, his bony shoulder protruding from the pale blue *yucata*. Angelica closed the door hurriedly. How dreadful, she thought, you can't lock any doors here!

At last she discovered her stockings in a sort of rack standing on the mat, and proceeded to pull them on, balancing like a lean heron first on one leg then on the other. The low mirror of the dressing table reflected the image of a leg cut off at mid-thigh; she moved away, shocked. She could not understand why Brownley had announced with a laugh, the night before, that he thought these mirrors very convenient. But how could she go out without her clothes? She'd have to make do with the brown padded kimono which the maid had thrust on her when she first came. Resigned, she bundled herself into it as best she could, and made her way along the corridor to the front door. Here another problem faced her. What had become of the shoes she had taken off on her arrival? These Japanese houses were infuriating. You couldn't find anything anywhere! She hunted in vain; then, by the doorstep, she saw several pairs of curious wooden clogs in a row—*geta*, that nice Miyamoto had called them. She picked up a pair, somewhat suspiciously; they were simply wooden soles mounted on two short vertical bars and fastened to the foot by a strap passing between the big toe and its neighbor. She tried them on, and tottered out into the garden, several inches taller. Two sparrows breakfasting beside the little mossy bridge took her for their old enemy, the rickety scarecrow in the nearby rice field, and flew swiftly away over the bamboo.

The boom of a gong sounded close by. Its deep sonorous vibrations ran through the dense shrubbery and around the house. A second note rang out, then another, a whole series growing faster and more insistent like a call to arms. Angelica started. The sound was coming from a large building adjoining the garden. In front of it, in the middle of the gravel courtyard, rose a monumental stone statue. "Buddha!" Angelica said to herself. "A temple! O Lord, I thank Thee for bringing Thine enemies within Thy servant's reach! If this be a test, O Lord, I shall show myself worthy of Thy trust!" Tottering on her *geta*, twisting her ankles, stumbling over every pebble, she rushed forward and made her way into the precincts of the temple. In front of the Buddha lay three oranges on a lacquer tray, an early-morning offering.

"Are you going to eat them?" Angelica taunted the Buddha. A deep humming sound, growing ever fainter, filled the air around her like some supernatural echo. Under a lean-to roof of gray tiles the gong was still quivering. She stood motionless in the middle of the courtyard.

From the depths of the temple came the sound of shuffling feet, and the shrill tinkle of a tiny bell. A man with a shaven head, draped in a yellow robe, appeared in the covered way that circled the temple—a fat man, holding a wooden rosary in his clasped hands. Behind him a procession of bonzes in black and yellow robes, their shaven heads gleaming, marched in silence. Nobody noticed the solitary stranger. They disappeared through an open doorway. There was a clash of cymbals, and a monotonous chant rose upward to the Buddhist deity accompanied by the click of a wooden clapper.

"O Lord," murmured Angelica, "let not these heathen voices rise in ignorant prayer toward their false gods! Forbid it, Lord!" She was in tears; somehow this exotic chant in the peaceful garden moved her in spite of herself. "Forbid it, I be-

66

seech Thee!" she repeated, and fell to her knees in deep distress, unaware that she was uttering her prayer at the feet of the stone Buddha. A hand on her shoulder roused her from her prostration; a bonze stood there in his priestly robes, watching her with a kindly smile. He spoke a few incomprehensible words and led her into the hall of prayer, motioning her to take off her *geta* before entering. There she saw each monk kneeling before a small black lacquer table, and the abbot in the midst with his back turned, on a red cushion. The bonze led her a little apart and brought her a cushion, smiling and attentive toward this unexpected disciple discovered at the feet of Buddha.

Angelica pulled herself together. She had followed the priest automatically, convinced that this invitation revealed the will of God, that He was making her task easier by setting her in the midst of the ungodly. She was even tempted to consider the whole course of that morning's events as miraculous, except that the New Baptists do not believe in miracles. She cast a critical eye around the room in which she was kneeling among those tonsured men, and was horrified by its orderly beauty. Dozens of silver pots were set out in rows on a huge low table; symbolic flowers stood in vases, a red lotus on the right hand, a yellow lotus on the left. Bronze lamps were everywhere, glowing dimly as if for some Byzantine orgy, and, what shocked her particularly, two Biblical-looking oil lamps. A bundle of small sticks in a large vessel close to the abbot gave out a pungent smell of incense which filled the room and made her head heavy. She detested the oriental odor of incense, more fit for the harem than for the house of prayer; the last time such a scent had offended her nostrils had been at the wedding of a distant cousin, a Roman Catholic. The priests' rich vestments, the carpeted chancel, the fine lace cloths on the altar, the massed flowers and the gilded statues, the profane music of violins from the organ loft, all came back to her at that moment, especially the wafts of incense scattered through the church by choirboys in red robes . . . red robes, yellow robes, incense, gongs, violins! Angelica was transported with wrath; she yearned for the plain black cross, the more moving for its bareness, that hung, unspoiled by indecent ornaments, on the white wall of the New Baptist Church of Burke City. What, she thought, am I doing kneeling among these idolators? She rose to her feet, an awe-inspiring figure in her brown kimono, her soul stern as the avenging angel's.

The abbot gave three taps on a small gong. A bonze seized a pair of wooden drumsticks and struck them together at regular intervals like a metronome. Tick tock, tick tock . . . Namu-Amida-Butsu, Namu-Amida-Butsu, the endless repetition of Buddha's name in token of faith in his great mercy. The priests' voices took it up in canon, as they did each morning, that this sacred invocation might flow in an unbroken stream of fervor. Angelica backed as far as the open door that gave on to the covered way, deliberately withdrawing from the heathen ceremony. "O Lord," she said aloud, "Thou mayest allow it in Thy great mercy, but I cannot endure it!" At the sound of this foreign voice, the monks' chorus wavered slightly. Then, mingling with the Namu-Amida-Butsu, there arose in that Buddhist temple the strangest chant ever heard there since the foundation of the sanctuary in 867.

> "Onward, Christian soldiers,
> Marching as to war,
> With the cross of Jesus
> Going on before."

Angelica stood transfigured, singing at the top of her voice, glaring ferociously at a tiny black statue of Buddha lurking in a dark corner. She had not intended to create a scene, but her zeal had made her forget that others besides her God were listening. Hear me, O Lord, she thought, and look down in Thy great goodness on these heathen monks wallowing in their ignorance.

A great to-do arose among the aforesaid heathen. While the bulk of the company resumed their incantations even more vociferously, two bonzes rose from their places and moved firmly toward the intruder. Angelica did not flinch. Oppor-

68

tunely remembering the second verse, she sang even louder. Her sublime notes rang out above the impious prayer, the rattle of the drumsticks and the clash of cymbals which had now joined in:

> "At the sign of triumph
> Satan's legions flee;
> On then, Christian soldiers,
> On to victory.
> Hell's foundations quiver
> At the shout of praise . . ."

The two priests, perhaps subdued by this aggressive blast of sound, consulted one another swiftly.

"Who is this honorable lunatic?" asked the first.

"I found her kneeling before the Buddha in the garden. We have some disciples in foreign lands; no doubt she is praying in her own fashion."

"We shall have to teach her; meanwhile it is not seemly that she should be allowed to shout thus."

They moved forward gently, their hands hidden in their long sleeves, and bowed in unison repeatedly, hoping that this demonstration of politeness would force her to follow suit according to Japanese custom, and thus put an end to her praiseworthy but highly disturbing profession of faith. Unfortunately, Angelica did not know the rules of the game.

"Begone, you slaves of Satan! Don't you touch me! I tell you, in the name of the Lord who hears me and helps me, Beelzebub shall reign no longer over this garden of transgression."

The words were obscure and rhapsodic, but conveyed an unshakable resolve. Uttering them like an anathema, Angelica flung both arms heavenward, just as she had done as a girl when playing the part of the prophet Isaiah in Sunday school pageants. Her movement was too sudden or too enthusiastic, or maybe the Devil wanted to prove that he meant to defend himself; at all events, Angelica's kimono flew open. The priests found themselves peering at a white-skinned body, somewhat gaunt perhaps but very different from those of their wives. They rose slowly, staring with impassive concentration. "Satan!" cried Angelica, and, turning on her heels, fled from the accursed temple. Down the garden paths she ran, barefooted, disheveled, haggard, tears pouring down her cheeks.

Beside the little pond she paused to take breath and collect herself. From the temple she could hear the muffled clash of cymbals as the prayer got under way once more. "The battle will be long and full of snares," she said to herself, glaring intently at the graceful curve of the temple roof. She reached home at last, to find the house quietly asleep. Only a maid sweeping out the doorway greeted her with a smile. Angelica tried to explain, by scratching the palm of her hand with one finger, that she was anxious to write. The girl, conditioned to do whatever was asked of her, especially by foreigners, seized the older woman's hand and tickled her palm with a merry laugh— What an odd way of saying good morning! she thought—Angelica blanched; to be touched so, with such familiarity! Would her ordeals never end?

"No," she said, "some writing paper, don't you see, writing paper . . ."

She traced out letters on the wall. The maid eventually understood and brought her a pad and a pencil. Angelica wrote out in block capitals:

EXPRESS CABLE.

TO: DAVID WOLF

   NEW BAPTIST CHURCH

   BURKE CITY, SOUTH DAKOTA, U.S.A.

AM IN THICK OF BATTLE AMONG LEWD AND UNGODLY JAPANESE. URGENTLY NEED SUPPORT FROM PRAYERS OF BRETHREN AND SISTERS. THE LORD SHALL PREVAIL. LETTER FOLLOWS.

                       ANGELICA

As she finished, Mr. Miyamoto appeared in the doorway, as full of early-morning cheerfulness as a canary.

"Miyamoto," she called to him. "Can you take this cable for

me right away? It's most urgent. Give them the address for the reply, I don't even know where I am."

Mr. Miyamoto took the sheet of paper and went out. "She might at least have said *Mr.* Miyamoto," he grumbled to himself.

It was an hour later when Liliane Laage awoke, and noticed that the cat which had spent the night at the end of her *futon* had disappeared. She called Keiko San, who came in carrying a tray laden with breakfast: soya soup, pickled turnips, raw fish, rice, seaweed and unsweetened green tea. She had changed her plum-colored kimono for a plain blouse and skirt. She looked quite pretty, thought Liliane, although she had lost her exotic charm. Moreover, pickled turnips seemed singularly unappetizing at 8 A.M. Liliane munched a couple of turnips and drank a few mouthfuls of tea, then decided to get dressed. Keiko San, faithful to the Japanese ritual of the daily bath, which had been allowed to lapse on the previous night, led her to the *o furo*. She emerged from this thoroughly cleansed but rather on edge, and this again seemed all wrong at that hour of day.

"Have you seen the cat?" Liliane asked as she donned flannel slacks and a close-fitting red sweater.

"Neko San—Mr. Cat?" the girl replied. "We will look for him."

Mme. Hashi, whom they consulted, declared that the cat had been seen hurrying toward the neighboring houses. Liliane and Keiko set off in search of it, the Japanese girl delighted with this pretext for showing off the elegant Frenchwoman about whom she had so much to tell.

The first person they met was an old woman bent double by the weight of seventy years of humility. Armed with a pail of water, she was sluicing the beaten earth roadway in front of her house. She would have to repeat this operation five or six times in the course of the day, like millions of other Japanese women, in an endless battle against the dust that rises from the roads and filters through the ill-fitting paper windows. She regarded the

Frenchwoman with suspicion, even with hostility, recognizing a newcomer to the district. Keiko San told her everything: the midnight arrival of the travelers, Liliane's bath, the splendor of her clothes, the texture of her skin and the raw fish served her for breakfast. This last tid-bit decided the poor woman to ask what she could do for the honorable visitor. Keiko San replied that her companion was a Frenchwoman on a visit to Japan, and launched into a description of France in which singers, writers, poets and film stars featured largely. Liliane caught the names of Matissou, Sartrou, Bligitte Bardot.

The old woman, although well acquainted with the inn cat, inquired anxiously as to its color, sex, eyes, size, weight, demeanor, ancestry and character—after which she announced that she was very sorry she had not seen it. This was untrue, for she was really much relieved to have been spared an encounter with so sinister an animal, which kills a woman and then assumes her shape. For the cat, apart from the serpent, is the only creature that showed no distress at the bedside of the dying Buddha, and hence is an object of contempt to those survivors of an older generation who, like this old woman, are steeped in folklore.

Neko San turned up at the next house, the home of *Sensei* (or Master) Zengo Asaki. Here Keiko San repeated her speech to a maid sweeping out the tiny garden. She adorned it further with picturesque details about the Frenchwoman's way of cleaning her teeth, brushing her eyelashes and rubbing perfumed toilet water on her bosom. Liliane gathered from the maid's curious glances that they were talking about her, and knew that after two conversations of such length no detail of her person would be hidden from the local inhabitants. The young maid went off to inform her master, with a great deal of giggling, that two women, one of them a foreigner, were waiting in his garden. He got the whole story, raw fish, toilet water and the rest, accompanied by a meticulous description of the stranger's person. The *Sensei*, a man of about thirty, well-built and tall for a Japanese, listened with half-shut eyes and resolved to have a closer look at this woman. Meanwhile Liliane, with the cat in her arms, suggested going home, for she felt this exhibition had lasted long enough.

"Oh no," said Keiko San, "that would not be polite. We must thank the *Sensei* first."

Liliane went through the front door and was about to cross the step which, in Japanese houses, indicates the inviolable threshold.

"No, that would not be polite," repeated Keiko San. "We must wait here."

At this crisis, Master Asaki appeared. He knelt down close to the edge of the doorstep, leaving his visitors standing—a method which enables the Japanese to receive guests without asking them in. The host is at his ease, while the visitors, left standing, are forced to cut short their call. Keiko San at once produced a new edition of the story which Asaki had already heard from his maid. This gave him ample time for a secret scrutiny of the strange woman. Liliane Laage had dark hair and black eyes and a neat, pretty little nose, which was as well since the Japanese think blond hair barbarous and long noses grotesque, while light-colored eyes remind them of fish. Moreover, she was not tall. The *Sensei* noted all of this.

"This is Master Asaki," announced Keiko San.

"Oh really? Master of what?"

"*Karate*, Japanese fighting."

"Oh, Judo?" said Liliane. And she recalled the exploit of the Judo champion who floored his adversary merely by whispering something in his ear.

"No, not Judo; *karate!*"

The Master smiled, and proceeded to slice the air with his hand in great whirling movements until Liliane realized that he was demonstrating a kind of sport in which the opponents fight with the side of the hand instead of weapons.

Asaki said something. "The Master is going to demonstrate for you," Keiko San interpreted.

73

Asaki went out into the garden, picked up five tiles from a heap, laid them one above the other like a little wall, and split all five of them with one blow. Liliane clapped her hands and had a closer look at the tile-splitter. She found him oddly attractive, with his muscular frame, broad shoulders, powerful neck and shaven head. She gave him her sweetest smile which greatly pleased the *Sensei*, though the close-fitting red sweater pleased him even more. He launched into a long peroration the gist of which, as translated by Keiko San, was that he could easily break fifteen or twenty tiles at one blow and would be delighted to prove this by and by to the honorable visitor. So, as the two women made their way back to the inn, Keiko San pondering a fresh problem: the *Sensei* had behaved with discreet politeness, without that exaggerated courtesy which a Japanese displays toward guests whom he has no intention of seeing again. The subtle nuance did not escape her. "*Sensei* Asaki must be in love!" she said, and laughed.

Liliane smiled, too, but the suggestion lingered in her mind.

Nicole Marchand went out that morning too, but she went alone, intending to take a leisurely walk through the unfamiliar surroundings. Leaving the pretty houses near the inn, she turned down the first lane she came to and passed, first of all, a long row of huts huddled together in chaotic disorder, looking like hen-houses or garden sheds. The dusty roadway was full of bumps and ruts and lacked pavements or gutters. Telegraph poles planted along the road haphazardly held a tangled skein of sagging wires at roof-height. The timber of the houses was shabby with wear and weather, without the dignity of age. The paper *shoji* on the windows, drably gray and often torn or patched with pages torn from magazines, told their wretched tale of poverty. In fact everywhere, the squalid poverty of the crowded slum met her eyes, and she realized that the Japan she knew from posters and writers had vanished once she crossed the threshold of the inn. Worse still, the tattered *shoji*, the threadbare mats, the broken roofs patched with sheet iron, the sickly-looking foliage in the tiny gardens thickly coated with gray dust, were actually grotesque vestiges of Japan's famous picturesqueness. Nicole recalled the dazzling posters put out by travel agencies and airline companies, which showed smiling women in red kimonos posed against a background of dolls' houses. She recognized these posters here, their color washed out and blurred into a pervading drabness, half torn down by the grim wind of truth, like some derelict advertisement hanging from a ruined wall.

Nicole walked for a long time, turning now right, now left, plunging deeper at every step into this unending slum. And it was indeed unending. Here and there stood a pretty house which she scarcely noticed, so greatly did the neighboring huts oppress her with their ugliness. The streets through which she wandered swarmed with ill-clad men and women in threadbare, tattered Western dress, worn-out *geta* on their bare feet; here and there, she saw a woman in a kinomo, but they were few and far between, for these expensive garments are little worn among the working classes.

An intolerable stench went by in the wake of a handcart, on which stood a dozen closed barrels; a man in a cotton tunic stopped in front of a house, seized one of the barrels and went off to empty the cesspool. Peasant women in baggy trousers who had come in early that morning from their villages were dragging another cart which they filled with garbage. Nicole came at last to a market thronged with housewives. She took note of their meager purchases—a piece of dried fish here, a chunk of fish pulp there, a few salted cabbages, a single apple. She watched their thick red hands counting out ten-yen pieces, one by one, as if they were gold coins. She stood there for a long time, stunned at the sight of that long procession of poor folk, creeping like ants out of their hovels. It seemed to her at that moment the essential and unforgettable image of Japan.

Two dazzling cherry trees in full bloom stood out in isolated brightness against that dark setting. A crowd was gazing at them, pressing close to them as if there were something miraculous about the two trees. Nicole realized why Japanese cherry trees, which are no different from those in the West and indeed are less plentiful, have assumed such importance in the eyes of the whole world. It is because their transient splendor is chiefly striking by contrast with a background of black squalor and destitution.

IV

A Trying Week for Miyamoto

———

Sunday

   Cadwallader sent for Miyamoto first thing in the morning. Their interview marked the beginning of a series of adventures into which the clients of the Agency dragged the poor young man between visits to temples and night clubs. Following Germain's instructions, and faithful to the code of honor which governs the relations between a Japanese subordinate and his superiors, Miyamoto flung himself into these adventures almost to his own undoing, until the day when a high-placed police official summoned him to remember that he was, after all, a Japanese. But let us not anticipate . . .

Cadwallader came straight to the point. "How many geishas are there in Tokyo?"

"About two hundred," replied Miyamoto, "reckoning only those of the best class."

"Two hundred women held in conditions of slavery! What was MacArthur doing all those six years?" the American wondered aloud. "Do you think you could get them all together for me?" he asked. "The sooner the better. I've barely three weeks ahead of me."

Miyamoto knew something about geishas, for a young cousin of his was a member of that honorable body. Without asking himself pointless questions, he made a mental reckoning. A dozen were mistresses of V.I.P.'s, thirty or forty of high officials or big capitalists, fifty refused point-blank to have anything to do with foreigners . . .

He replied cautiously, "You may be able to choose between about eighty geishas, Mr. Cadwallader."

"I didn't say choose," the American cut in sharply, "I said all together. Can you fix that for me?"

Mr. Miyamoto had acquired the Western habit of answering promptly, but this question left him stunned. What was the American after, and what boundless wealth must he possess? Eighty geishas at once! This was something quite unprecedented, . . . utterly impossible. But how could he disillusion Cadwallader without failing in politeness and going against the wishes of his employer? He tried an indirect attack:

"Excuse my indiscretion, Mr. Cadwallader, but dinners with honorable geishas are extremely expensive. There would be the geishas' fees, tips for the waitresses and the proprietress of the restaurant, as well as the cost of the dinner, with sake and taxis and presents for your guests—"

"I never mentioned any guests apart from the geishas. I will be there and you will be my interpreter, that's all."

For all his impassivity, Mr. Miyamoto jumped. The honorable American wants eighty geishas for himself . . . and me! The last of the shoguns himself never gave such a party as that!

"A geisha dinner just for yourself," he asked incredulously, "have I understood you correctly?"

There was admiration in his voice.

"Who said dinner?" cut in Cadwallader. "If you think it's necessary we can order refreshments to make the atmosphere more friendly, but nothing more. I just want a get-together—

in the big room at the inn for instance—where these girls and I can have a heart-to-heart talk."

Mr. Miyamoto's admiration dwindled. What a way to speak! Refreshments, heart-to-heart, the inn parlor—for the flower of Japanese womanhood!

He stared down at the mat and said with great earnestness, "Geishas are very much in request, it would be difficult and quite contrary to traditional etiquette to trouble them for anything less than a dinner party."

Cadwallader thought the Japanese was skeptical of his bank account, an intolerable suspicion for a proud citizen of Chicago.

"I've several thousand dollars in the Bank of Tokyo, which the League of which I am President has transferred to me for the expenses of my inquiry. I'm not afraid of costs, and if you feel a traditional dinner is indispensable, it's O.K. by me. It's all the same. I can give my talk during dinner. But I need to know the date right away."

This was an order. Mr. Miyamoto thought it as well to point out that the ladies could not possibly be invited to the inn. Special restaurants called *o-chaya*, honorable teahouses, organized such dinner parties, and geishas never accepted invitations to supper in private houses, except for a few palaces which had escaped the American democratic reform.

"O.K., O.K.," Cadwallader said wearily, "I'll leave you to fix the restaurant, whichever you like. You'll need some money to get things started, how much would you like? A thousand dollars?"

Miyamoto quickly translated the sum into yen—three hundred and sixty thousand! The man must be a *daimio* in his own country!

"Excuse me a moment," he said, "I must put through a call."

He lifted the receiver of the telephone that stood on the mat and launched into long explanations in his own tongue. At the other end of the wire Miss Cloudless Sky made a face, while assuring her cousin of her humble and wholehearted devotion. An American tourist? She showed little enthusiasm. People like that

79

understood nothing, turned up in extraordinary dress, and talked all during the Shikoku Fishermen's Dance, the prettiest of all. The last time she had accepted an American invitation to dinner her hosts had even laughed at her white make-up. She'd been obliged to laugh heartily herself, though she had felt like crying. For nothing on earth would she repeat such an experience!

"Very awkward," Miyamoto translated. "My cousin the geisha says that she and all her friends are booked up for the whole week."

"Raise the price," yelled the American, irked by this chatter. "Back home in Chicago we'd have it all fixed by now."

Miyamoto picked up the receiver again. "I shall be there myself," he told his cousin. "The dinner is being given for the honorable Mr. Cadwallader and myself. We want the best *o-chaya*, with all your friends and your friends' friends. The honorable host is extremely rich and represents a very powerful society. . . ."

Miss Cloudless Sky, reassured by the prospect of her cousin's company, changed her mind. She promised to speak about it to Mama San and then call back.

"Who on earth is Mama San?" asked Cadwallader, sensing that the affair was getting rather complicated.

"Mama San is the head of the *Geishaya* where my cousin lives. My cousin can decide nothing without her permission. We shall have to await her answer."

Twenty minutes later Mama San called back. She never, she explained, accepted offers from foreigners, but she would make an exception in favor of the friend of Miss Cloudless Sky's cousin. Miyamoto announced this triumphantly. Cadwallader thanked him, raging inwardly, for he had grasped the identity of Mama San, even as the latter went on to protest her boundless enthusiasm for the scheme, provided that the honorable American allowed her to organize the dinner. She suggested three regular geishas, two assistants to pour out sake, and four *maikos* or apprentices, to dance.

"What?" stormed the President of the Sons of the American

80

Revolution. "I don't want a private orgy, I want to get information, and if there has to be a dinner I want the greatest possible number of geishas."

"My honorable friend," said Miyamoto into the telephone, "takes a discreet interest in the admirable traditions which have brought the geishas their world-wide fame. He humbly desires the privilege of meeting a large number of them that evening. Everything is to be of the best—the most select restaurant, the finest kimonos, the most exquisite dances. This dinner party for honorable geishas is the chief object of his journey here, the most keenly desired . . ."

The little man grew lyrical, impelled by the longing to get things settled.

Mama San smelled gold. In Akasaka, the geisha district, telephone wires hummed. A super-rich American, infatuated with Japan, was treating himself to the most sensational geisha party seen in years. "Yes, of course," added the proprietress of Miss Cloudless Sky, "we have a free hand to organize as we like." A score of Mama Sans exclaimed that their geishas were unworthy of so great an honor—which meant that they accepted without hesitation. The telephone line to the Pine Wind Inn was engaged for several hours, as the ladies eagerly sought more information. The proprietress of the honorable teahouse talked for twenty-five minutes. Mr. Miyamoto was so overwhelmed by assurances of respectful admiration that he quite forgot the American. The Misses Rosy Glow, Morning Mist, Murmuring Wind, Mountain Pine, Spring Snow and others with equally poetic names telephoned the inn in turn. The five maids of the inn, attracted by the ceaseless tinkle of the telephone bell, came to kneel by Miyamoto's side and drink in every word of the conversation. In the end twenty-five geishas accepted. The dinner was to take place the following Thursday and would cost three thousand dollars.

Cadwallader drew a checkbook from his pocket. He scribbled out the requisite sum plus a hundred dollars, offered the check to Miyamoto and said: "I've made it out to bearer, you can cash it at the Bank of Tokyo and keep the balance for yourself."

81

The little Japanese protested: people like himself never accepted tips, particularly if their father had been a general. And at last the baffled American took back his check, and made out another for three thousand exactly. Miyamoto pocketed this promptly, calculating how much would be gratefully refunded by the restaurant and the Mama Sans. A Japanese is always willing to accept a present if it is made according to the rules.

The news of this monster dinner party spread like wildfire through Tokyo. The five maids at the inn, the twenty Mama Sans, the twenty-five geishas and the proprietress of the teahouse announced it like a communiqué of victory—a party costing a million yen! Inevitably Sato San, Chief of the Aliens Branch of the Tokyo Police, heard of it from his girl friend Miss Morning Mist and from the Superintendent of the district where the inn stood who himself had the news from a policeman who was courting one of the maids. He made a note of the date: Thursday, April 11th.

Monday

Miss Angelica Simpson was gazing into the garden when a man in a gray robe entered it from the temple next door. She recognized the bonze who had taken her into the oratory, and hastily closed the *shoji* of her bedroom. Then, realizing that this unfriendly action was likely to cut short a contact which might prove fruitful to the cause of her faith, she opened the window again and gave a noncommittal smile. The monk bowed and went into the house. Minutes later Mr. Miyamoto, having been notified by the maid, knocked at Miss Simpson's door and announced that the honorable Prior of the Temple of Z——, Toyota San, desired to see her. Mme. Hashi, he added, had suggested that the interview take place in one of the large ground-floor rooms, more befitting the dignity of the visitor, who had already been shown into it. Angelica, wearing a severely cut brown suit of good woolen cloth, followed the young Japanese.

Toyota San was waiting beside a long low table of red lacquer. Miyamoto had never met him before, and therefore greeted him with deliberate and formal courtesy. He knelt down three yards away from the bonze, laid his forearms on the mat and bent forward until his head was touching his hands. The monk followed suit with remarkable agility. They exchanged rarefied compliments. Angelica, decidedly ill at ease, stood apart, wondering how she herself was to greet this prostrate figure. At last Mr. Miyamoto stood up and made the requisite introductions first in Japanese and then in French. The monk touched the ground with his forehead several times; Angelica resignedly held out her hand and made a slight bow, which obliged the monk to rise to his feet. Then, at a sign from Miyamoto, the three of them knelt round the table. The bonze was invited to take the place of honor with his back to the *tokonoma*. A maid brought green tea and small tasteless pink cakes that appeared to be made of compressed sawdust. And with his third cup of tea the honorable Prior Toyota San embarked on a dissertation about the beauty of the garden. Miyamoto realized that the motive of his call must be a serious and delicate one.

"What's he saying?" asked Angelica.

"He says that the garden is particularly pleasant at this time of year."

"Oh," said Angelica.

The monk went on speaking, while Miyamoto nodded approval. Ten minutes elapsed.

"What's he saying?" repeated Angelica.

"He says that the trees are greener than last year."

"Oh," said Angelica again, more than a little astonished that the monk should call on her to discuss the beauties of Nature.

The conversation went on between the two Japanese, each waiting for his interlocutor to pause in order to begin talking himself. Ten more minutes elapsed.

"What *is* he saying?" demanded Angelica.

"He says that the cherry trees in this garden are among the finest in Tokyo."

Angelica made a great effort. "Come to think of it," she said, "I don't suppose you could find prettier cherry trees."

Mr. Miyamoto interpreted. As if he had only been waiting for this judicious comment to bring the interview to a close, Toyota San rose, declaring that this delightful conversation with so distinguished a lady afforded him indescribable pleasure. Miyamoto pricked up his ears. These parting words had at last given him an inkling of the motive behind the monk's visit. Even more earnestly, he replied that Miss Simpson was deeply appreciative of the honorable Prior's kindness in calling on her.

"Please be so good as to tell this lady," the monk went on, "that we shall always be highly honored to receive her in the temple of Z—— and that I shall take the greatest pleasure in perfecting her already extensive knowledge of Buddhist worship."

Completely at a loss, Miyamoto repeated this announcement word for word. It took Angelica's breath away, which enabled the monk to make his way to the door.

"My goodness," she gasped at last, "what's he thinking of? I'm not a Buddhist. My God is the Christian God and no other; please tell him so straightaway."

Even more bewildered by this sibylline statement, Miyamoto lost his head and translated it literally, without thinking. Toyota San burst into loud, prolonged laughter, and with repeated thanks and bows strode off to his temple, understanding now that the intruder had indeed violated the sanctuary, far from reverencing it as he had thought at first. Miyamoto remained thoughtful. The whole business puzzled him, but he felt sure that the monk, who had come to make discreet inquiries, had left in a hostile mood for some mysterious reason largely connected with the American visitor. He cast an anxious glance at her.

"To think he took me for a Buddhist," she fumed. "I hope you told him I was a Christian? If you didn't I shall go straight to the temple."

He assured her that her wishes had been fulfilled, and then took his leave of this peculiar woman who, only six days after her arrival, had already incurred the enmity of the honorable and powerful Prior of the Temple of Z——. As for Angelica, she shut herself in her room, sick with shame at having been so misunderstood by those dreadful monks. She was only roused from her thoughts by the arrival of a maid bearing a telegram. Angelica tore it open and read:

HAVE ASKED LORD TO ASSIST YOU. ADVISE PRUDENCE AS JAPANESE NOTORIOUSLY STUBBORN. TESTIFY TO THE FAITH AND TRUST IN THE LORD. YOU MAY COUNT ON OUR PRAYERS.

DAVID WOLF

How right he is, she thought; what wisdom and what faith! Testify, that's the thing, I must testify.

She pondered for a moment, then opened the door and called, "Mr. Miyamoto!"

He appeared dutifully.

"Mr. Miyamoto, find me two strong poles, one five yards long and the other two, some string and a pickax, and take them into the garden for me."

He understood less and less, but went off to hunt for the required objects. Like many country homes in Japan the inn had a large stock of bamboo sticks of different sizes. Miyamoto notified Mme. Hashi. Anticipating entertainment, she dispatched two maids armed with a saw and a pickax.

"Aren't these foreigners amusing?" she said to Miyamoto. "We must go and see what the honorable American lady is going to do."

The little man gave polite assent, though he felt somewhat uneasy about it all. Angelica had the bamboos cut to the length she wanted, seized the string and tied one piece across the other. "A cross!" Miyamoto said to himself, faint with horror as he understood. "She's mad, Toyota San will never allow that!"

Bamboo weighs very little. Angelica shouldered her cross without difficulty and set off for Golgotha, walking slowly with bent head. Mme. Hashi, Miyamoto and the maids stood rooted to the spot, spellbound by this extraordinary spectacle as she made her

85

way toward the temple. But quickly curiosity got the upper hand and they followed her, Miyamoto bringing up the rear. Reaching the clipped bush which marked the boundary between the garden and the temple grounds, Angelica laid down her cross and demanded the pickax. Now Miyamoto discreetly departed, dragging Mme. Hashi with him. Only the two maids remained, too slow-witted to sense danger. Angelica lifted her pickax and started making a deep hole. "He thought I was a Buddhist!" she muttered to herself between strokes. Her limbs ached from the effort and sweat poured down her forehead. Then, raising the cross, she planted it in the hole facing the temple so that it rose a good three feet above the bush. A monk who had heard the crash of the pickax appeared in the cloister of the temple. The maids took to their heels; Angelica watched them, a taste of dust and ashes in her mouth.

The honorable Toyota San, Prior of the temple, glared venomously at this impertinent cross, went back to his office and picked up the telephone.

At the other end of the line, Sato San, Chief of the Aliens Branch of the Tokyo Police, assured Toyota San of his respectful devotion. Then he stared pensively into the void, reflecting that the Pine Wind Inn was a bit too much in the news.

Tuesday

Liliane Laage drank another cup of green tea. Beside her, a silent Zengo Asaki was staring vacantly at the mat, his shaven head gleaming in the light that filtered through the *shoji*.

The door into the next room was ajar and Liliane caught sight of an unfolded *futon*. She had acquired enough familiarity with Japanese ways to know that at five o'clock in the afternoon the bedding normally has not yet been taken out of its cupboard. In any case she had quite clearly understood the point of this invitation to drink a cup of tea, which Keiko San, wriggling with excitement, had brought her that morning. "Master Asaki is in love!" the girl had said once again.

She got up, for she knew he would never dare, and pretending to explore the room, pushed the half-open door and went into the other room. He followed her. For a few seconds they stood face to face, then without more ado he flung her down on the *futon*. Liliane thought his method somewhat abrupt but reflected that, given the language difficulty, there was no other solution. The man was wearing an indoor kimono which gave a generous glimpse of his muscular thighs, olive-skinned and smooth. Encouraged by what she saw, Liliane allowed herself to be undressed. Her body was white—very white underneath her red sweater. He stared at her, his face blank. For one brief instant she was frightened. He looked like some barbarian warrior from the Asiatic hordes of medieval times. She recalled some story about horsemen who dried their meat between their legs and their horses' cruppers. The thought made her giggle. She stroked the top of his head lightly. The close-shorn hair tickled her palm, like a day's growth of beard. "You're quite attractive, my little Mongol," she told him with a smile. "Your eyes are fine when you condescend to open them, and I like you when you make your Genghis Khan face."

Asaki stood over the *futon*, pronounced a few guttural words in Japanese and pounced roughly on her. It was all over in barely a minute. Liliane waited for a little, then got up, donned her clothing and lit a cigarette. Asaki was still lying there, and she looked down at him.

"You were in a bit of a hurry, my little Mongol! Can it be that you're still primitive, for all your ancient Japanese civilization?"

She felt cheated, and wanted to get away from this strange creature. "Come on, get up," she said at last.

She felt that she was undeniably the stronger of the two. As she stood there, Asaki's room suddenly seemed to shrink. If she raised her arm she could touch the ceiling. Everything looked small to her—the bare room, the *futon* in the middle, the garden no bigger than a cabbage patch, Asaki himself, now belching and clearing his throat. Liliane went out, wondering how on earth she could have yielded so quickly to such a creature—and a mediocre lover in the bargain. Asaki joined her in the garden. He had straightened his kimono and tied the wide sash which enhanced the narrowness of his hips and the breadth of his torso.

She took him by the hand and said, pointing to a heap of tiles, "Now's the time to show me how you can break ten of them." Picking up ten tiles, she made a pile of them: "Go ahead, strong man!" she said.

Asaki raised his hand and brought it down in a single sharp blow. Nine tiles were broken, the tenth remained intact. Liliane burst into uncontrollable laughter.

"You've bungled it, my little Mongol!"

She was still laughing when she reached the inn. Asaki watched her go, his heart seething with fury. He, the *karate* champion, revered by a whole generation of sportsmen, had failed to break his ten tiles in front of a woman! As soon as Liliane's elegant figure had vanished he stamped around his garden, roaring like a wounded lion. Wounded he was indeed, wounded in his pride. With the side of his hand he split the handle of a spade, bashed in a tin pail and cut his week's supply of firewood. Then, feeling somewhat calmer, he broke eleven tiles at one blow and left in a mood of serenity for the honorable public baths.

It was six o'clock in the afternoon. The street that led to the baths was full, as usual, of a stream of men and women in night-kimonos, clattering along on their wooden *getas*. They were going to enjoy a communal relaxation in huge tubs of scalding water, and above all to exchange the endless trivial gossip of the neighborhood. Asaki San paid fifteen yen and received in exchange a wicker basket in which he deposited his clothes, under the uninterested gaze of the female attendant. With his soap and towel in one hand, he dipped the other into various tubs, in search of the hottest. A hundred naked men of all ages were sprawling there. He knew them all. From the next room came the sound of women's laughter; one of the men shouted a bawdy joke for their benefit, and the laughs rang out more shrilly. Asaki, having been carefully washed, slid into the tub between two of his friends, Matsuko the camera vendor and Nakagawa San the doctor. Everyone was lying still, reveling in the scalding water, but meanwhile gossiping or talking business with his neighbors.

"Well, Asaki San," asked Matsuko, "what do *you* think of the new flower girl at the station?"

One man quoted an old proverb that set them all roaring with laughter: "*Women and floor mats are best when they're new!* . . . I shall have to take a closer look at her."

"I'm not interested," replied Asaki. "I'm too tired."

"Not too tired to take an interest in a girl, surely? We all know you, ha ha!"

"I don't need to just now . . . I've got something much better."

The whole group demanded the story. Asaki was reluctant to speak, and then he remembered that sneer at his failure to break the tenth tile. "She's a tourist from the Pine Wind Inn, a Frenchwoman." He described the incident in the crudest terms. Knowing that his compatriots looked askance at intimate relations with foreigners, he thought it as well to treat his own with casual bawdiness.

Comments were fired at him.

"Does she do it as well as a Japanese?"

"Don't you find a European woman disgusting?"

"I hope you beat her," said the doctor, whose daughter had been raped by an American soldier.

Somebody broke into an army song and they all took up the chorus, substituting Liliane's name, which they had learned from Asaki, for the heroine's. Lying in the water they all bawled out: "And Lilianou San . . ." *Sensei* Asaki, the hero of the occasion, improvised several verses. They had a wonderful time. For in a confused way they knew that Asaki's success avenged their country for those tens of thousands of GI's who strolled along the streets of Tokyo arm in arm with Japanese girls.

Mr. Miyamoto, alone in a corner of the neighboring tub, listened in silence. He had escaped from the inn for a few minutes to relax from his troubles in the nearest public bath. The song surprised and shocked him, although he had heard from his sister about Mlle. Laage's visits to Asaki. Still he was mortified—mortified by the blow to the dignity of a woman for whom he felt responsible during her visit to Japan, but above all by the blow to his own dignity. For he felt a certain identity with his group of Westerners. He did not really care about the Frenchwoman's honor, and in any other circumstances he might have joined in the mocking chorus. But to hear lampoons in a public *furo* about somebody who was now his ally—this was shaming, this was past endurance. The verses of the infamous ballad flowed on until Asaki's departure. And Mr. Miyamoto, crouching in a corner of the bath all by himself, his head wreathed in steam, livid, vowed to have it out with Master Asaki without delay. When the time came he would show himself resolute, if only to prove Westerners do not have a monoply on gallantry.

Having made up his mind, he closed his eyes and sank back into water up to his chin.

Wednesday

"I've seen enough *torii* and museums these last three days," General de Lure remarked that morning. "Where do you propose to take us today?"

Germain thought the time was ripe for sending the general in search of military history.

"To Nikko, in the mountains north of Tokyo."

He recited in a weary neutral tone, "This temple was built in 1616 by Master Carpenter Hidari Jingoro, by order of Shogun Tokugawa. Notice its five-pinnacled pagoda, its statues of guardian-kings, bronze lanterns, lustral wells, the lacquer horse, the Yomeimon Gate, and the cryptomerias, conifers and mosses of the nearby forest."

The general heaved a sigh. "No, *mon vieux,* no! Too much of a good thing. You're taking us round this country as if it were a museum. What about the people themselves, don't you take them into account? Today I'm going to leave you and explore by myself."

"But you'll get lost, sir!"

"That doesn't matter. When I've had enough I shall hail a taxi and say Matsukaze Hotel. They tell me these taxi drivers are wonderful."

Germain shuddered at the thought of the general handed over defenseless to the infamous taxi drivers of Tokyo. Usually cabbies take you on a wild-goose chase lasting an hour or two. Honor satisfied, they finally admit their ignorance of your destination and hand you over to a smiling colleague who, in his turn, will satisfy honor by dragging you on another journey, and will give you up when darkness falls to a third driver who'll lose you completely.

"I don't need Miyamoto, you can take him with you if you like. Have you visited the Temple of Yasukuni, sir?"

"*Another* temple!"

This is the inevitable cry, the desperate appeal of every tourist after three hectic days in Japan, the thought that keeps him glued to his stool at the bar with a drink in his hand and a pretty slant-eyed hostess at his side.

"It's the temple of the demigods, of soldiers who fell in battle, where the spirits of heroes are assembled, among others that of General Miyamoto. His son might go with you. I've been there myself, and I found it rather moving."

Soldiers deified? Ah, the noble purity of the old way of life! thought the general. He had during the past ten years paid homage to the war memorials and Unknown Soldiers of all the great capitals of the world. In this pious pilgrimage he had only once been disappointed—at Panama City. Never having been at war, the good people of Panama had set up the indispensable mausoleum to the memory of . . . the Unknown Fireman.

The general settled for Yasukuni. Miyamoto went with him. In the taxi he reminisced about the cemeteries of Verdun and the heartbreaking grandeur of fields of wooden crosses. Miyamoto laughed nervously.

"So it's here," said General de Lure, standing motionless before the main building of the Temple of Yasukuni, "that your father's spirit lies at rest."

"According to our religion that is so, but I don't really believe it," said Miyamoto, although it was his firm conviction. "Emperors and priests have no power, surely, to order spirits to gather here. But in any event this is where I come to honor his memory."

"The dead of a defeated army are greater than the heroes of a victorious one," declared the general after a long silence.

He knew what he was talking about, and it was with an aching heart that he took off his hat and lowered his head in silent contemplation. He had stood thus hundreds of times during the course of his career, in respectful silence. Mr. Miyamoto admired the dignity of his pose.

They went out through the main *torii.* Two cripples in white tunics came up holding their begging bowls.

"Who are these unfortunate men?" asked the general, fumbling in his pocket. "War wounded, did you say?"

He was so used to questioning his own men about the quality of their rations or their loyal pride in the French army that he instinctively addressed the white-clad beggars: "Please tell them, *mon fils,* that a French general . . ."

The two beggars bowed down. You cannot talk to prostrate men whose faces are hidden, especially if you are a general. Those personal contacts between a leader and his men, which are so valuable and so inspiring, and moreover so necessary to the leader's self-esteem, become utterly impossible. The general broke off his speech and slipped into each bowl a crumpled five-hundred-yen note. A third beggar hurried up, his shoulders hunched above his crutches.

"It's disgraceful," said the general. "War victims shouldn't have to beg for a living!"

He pulled a thousand-yen note from his pocket and was about to give it to the newcomer when Miyamoto, in fits of laughter, seized it and, hiding it in the palm of his hand, ducked in a precipitate bow.

"What's come over you, *mon fils?* Have I done the wrong thing? Maybe a thousand yen was too much to give, but tell him that he owes me no gratitude, that from one soldier to another . . ."

Miyamoto was not listening; he was too busy exchanging orthodox salutations with the cripple. Each appeared delighted to meet the other and proffered long, polite phrases accompanied by innumerable bows.

"Every time I visit this temple, to which my wretched existence often brings me," the beggar was saying, "the memory of your glorious father General Miyamoto possesses me entirely. I shall never forget that I had the supreme honor of being present at his hara-kiri, which, alas, I failed to imitate as I should have wished."

"My family," Miyamoto replied, "is indebted to you for bringing back my father's ashes, and my honorable mother, who to her boundless sorrow was never able to express her deep gratitude to you, blessed your name with her dying lips."

Miyamoto's honorable mother would have been greatly surprised to hear this, for she had died ten years earlier in a state of unconsciousness, having lost her reason during the bombardment of Tokyo. The thousand-yen note was invisible, hidden in Miyamoto's hand. The general grew impatient.

"When you've quite finished, please be kind enough to let him have the money."

Mr. Miyamoto turned green, stammered incomprehensibly and bowed to the general, who wondered what had come over him. Finally he cleared his throat and said with an effort, "It's out of the question, sir, out of the question. We can't possibly give him this money without putting it in an envelope, and I've no envelope with me."

"Your tact is most commendable, but we were not so formal with the other soldiers."

Poor Miyamoto, on the verge of losing face, gave an agonized grin. This beggar was Hakayama San, the ex-lieutenant of the Imperial Army who had brought back Miyamoto's father and the ashes of his other superior officers from the Kuril Islands. Miyamoto wondered how to admit to a French general that this pitiful unshaven beggar was the officer who had held in his hands the funeral urn of General Miyamoto. To add to his confusion, people began to stare at the scene in surprise, puzzled at seeing such consideration shown to one of those miserable creatures—those constant reminders of the shame of defeat.

Hakayama San himself decided that the interview had gone on too long. He resented being an object of curiosity. Usually nobody even noticed him, and if he occasionally heard the chink of a coin in his bowl his invariable response was the inimitable Japanese bow which allowed him, without discourtesy, to hide his face and avert his eyes. For the past twelve years he had lived bowed down, ducking to the ground as soon as a passer-by drew near. Having suffered cruelly since his abortive suicide, he had never found courage to risk another attempt. He had been so bitterly ashamed of his cowardice and of his mendicant existence that he had ripped off his lieutenant's stars from his old military cap, choosing rather to forget—and to allow nobody, not even the other cripples who shared his room, to know—that he had once had the honor of being an officer. Having abolished that past, having wiped it from his memory, he subsided deeper into that abject state which was now the only one open to him, finding a sort of happiness in abasing himself twelve hours a day for the price of a liter of sake and three bowls of rice. Once in a while, the officer in him rebelled, as on that day when he turned his back on the American who had just taken his photograph and left him gaping with a hundred-yen note in his outstretched hand. Hakayama despised these impulses; they disturbed that inurement which alone makes degradation bearable. And now here was Miyamoto San, with a foreigner beside him, recognizing him despite his white tunic and greeting him with

94

the most formal politeness. Politeness is sheer mockery to a beggar.

The two Japanese simultaneously realized the falsity of their position and broke off their salutations. General de Lure sensed the constraint in the atmosphere, and asked bluntly, "Who *is* this man? You seem to know him."

Miyamoto thought quickly: Hakayama San begged for a living, true, but he had still borne an officer's rank when he took charge of the funeral urn. That alone mattered.

"Yes, I do know him. He is Hakayama San the beggar, the lieutenant of whom I told you on your first evening here."

General de Lure had a good memory. The suicide of a whole staff of officers after a defeat in battle was worth remembering.

"An officer! . . . Is it really possible?"

His amazement was so obvious, he seemed so painfully embarrassed, that the beggar, feeling the old sense of shame assail him once more, turned away without a word and hurried off as fast as his crutches would carry him.

"Run after him!" said the general. "We can't let him go like that. We must do something! You must at least give him those thousand yen . . . Oh no, of course, one of your father's officers . . . Well then, ask him his address, I'll go and visit him myself. I want to help him."

He was in real distress. True, a few minutes earlier he had been thinking what a fascinating story this encounter would make for his club members in Paris. Nevertheless he was deeply touched by the plight of this mendicant officer. He looked around and caught a last glimpse of the beggar turning a corner. Miyamoto stood as if turned to stone, bewildered by the tricky problems of protocol in which this chance meeting had involved him, incapable of deciding if he ought to consider the beggar as an officer or the officer as a beggar.

"Don't stand there gaping like an oaf," said the general, "don't you see we shall lose sight of him?"

"An oaf? What is an oaf?"

This unfamiliar word provided a heaven-sent diversion, and Miyamoto clung to it automatically. The general stared at him for some moments in amazement, noticed his sudden look of imbecility and muttering "To hell with the Japanese!" strode after the beggar. Miyamoto hesitated, cursing the tactlessness of foreigners. The general disappeared around the corner. Miyamoto, sick at heart, resigned himself to following him.

That morning, chance settled the fate of the ex-lieutenant. If he had turned right, he would have wandered into a maze of narrow lanes undisturbed by the hubbub of the city. Here he would easily have shaken off his well-meaning pursuers, and once they had vanished, his existence would have relapsed into that obscurity which alone made it endurable. But he turned left, into a huge avenue that was black with people.

An enormous crowd of men were assembled there, four or five thousand at least. All wore a white handkerchief knotted around their heads, the distinctive badge of the Japanese artisan. Perched on the platform of a van, a speaker with his sleeves rolled up clutched a megaphone and harangued the demonstrators in that solemn impassioned chant which gives such dramatic intensity to the most trivial Japanese speech. Hakayama San, still in flight, pushed through the crowd and reached the front row of listeners, who carried posters and streamers proclaiming in white letters on a red background: THE JAPANESE PEOPLE SAY NO TO AMERICAN BASES. In Tokyo, as in many other cities of the world the traditional scapegoat was receiving its periodic ration of insults.

At the climax of his speech the orator's voice was suddenly drowned by the scream of sirens. Ten great gray trucks screeched to a halt, blocking the whole width of the avenue. The dreaded Japanese police was launching an attack. Three hundred policemen in blue uniforms, with flat caps and chinstraps, their black rubber truncheons in their hands, charged the crowd, felling all those who opposed their advance. A few demonstrators resisted bravely. They were promptly struck to the ground, whereupon a fresh wave of attackers swept over them. Howls of pain could

96

be heard through the din. General de Lure, who had come into the avenue a few minutes before the police arrived, was swept up by the crowd in its flight and found himself in the neighborhood of the van, which was now deserted, the orator having fled to join the poster bearers in their disorderly retreat. At a guttural order from a police officer the van was overturned, crushing one of the demonstrators as it fell. Seized with panic, those who still offered some resistance flung down their posters and took to their heels, leaving behind them only a few wounded victims, the ex-lieutenant who, with his one leg, could not move fast enough, and General de Lure, astonished at finding himself in such a situation. One of the wounded men, whose head had been cut, was bleeding copiously; a policeman came up, probably intending to help him; the man lashed out in a frenzy and hit him in the face. This started off a final swift battle.

Hakayama San, caught up against his will in the struggle, found himself suddenly face to face with a policeman. He raised his arm in self-protection; the excited policeman brought down his truncheon and the beggar fell to the ground, unconscious. The general, who had witnessed the incident, rushed forward. And that, in a demonstration, was enough to prove him guilty. He had barely time to shout "Shame!" before being struck down in his turn. As he could not read Japanese and had understood nothing of the speech or the slogans, he did not even know in what cause he had fallen.

Which is the usual fate of soldiers.

Wednesday, *continued*

Germain set off for Nikko with the five other tourists, a polyglot guide from the Japanese Travel Bureau, and Keiko San in a cherry-red kimono. Thanks to the guide's learning, and more to his loquacity, Germain was free to devote all his attentions to the girl. The absence of her brother, whom Germain had cunningly dispatched with General de Lure, seemed to release Keiko from some secret constraint; during the entire train journey she never stopped talking and laughing. At every station she dragged Germain onto the platform in search of local delicacies. He thus swallowed in succession, at twenty-minute intervals, eel soup, a handful of uncooked dried beans, a roast sparrow soaked in *shoyu*, a boiled sea snail, three rounds of smoked cuttlefish and a sugared turnip. He felt rather sick but extremely happy. Three students in black jackets with gilt buttons came up to tell him how glad they were to make the acquaintance of a Frenchman. One of them drew from his pocket a volume of French poetry and very politely begged for a lesson in diction. How could one say no? Germain devoted himself for the rest of the journey to an explanation of the intricacies of French verse.

The pupils nodded their heads at each of his comments, and the less they understood the more they admired. But even without understanding they appreciated the music of the words, that rare harmony of the French language which appealed to the sentimental child latent within them—one of the many secret selves of every Japanese. Germain enjoyed reading aloud, and did not stop till he had reached the end of the book. Half the carriage was listening. People whispered that he was a *Sensei*. The passengers who got out bowed to him as they passed. Keiko San could not take her eyes off him. Then, as on every occasion when he felt himself engulfed in that typically Japanese current of soothing respect and continuous approbation, he was seized with an irresistible desire to pull their legs.

"The essential thing in French," he said, "is to know how to pronounce your words. We have certain typical phrases which students repeat every day for practice."

Keiko San interpreted. Their eyes lit up, and they begged for the magic formulae. Knowing the inability of the Japanese to pronounce the letter L, Germain brought out the cruel sentence: "Lucy Locket liked to lick her lovely lollipops."

The result was better than he had dared to hope. The next few minutes were irresistibly funny. The three students mingled their voices in a formless chant, repeating over and over again: "Rucy Rocketu riked . . . rovery rorripops," dribbling in their vain efforts to get their tongues around that impossible L.

"No, no," said Germain, "Lucy Locket liked . . ."

He rattled off the sentence, while they stared at him in anguish and chanted more earnestly than ever. He had to take refuge at the end of the car to laugh at his ease. The students worried over those lovely lollipops for a good half-hour, regardless and indeed unconscious of their own absurdity, and accompanied by a small crowd of travelers attracted by the noise and anxious for instruction. "Learning," had said Emperor Meiji, the mid-nineteenth century reformer, "shall be sought for among other nations of the world and the empire shall attain the zenith of prosperity." Whether their object be to build battleships or to pronounce lollipops, the Japanese have always shown the same inexhaustible zeal in pursuit of any scrap of information from foreign sources. On the station platform at Nikko, while the inevitable snapshot of Germain and the three students was being taken, the latter were still talking about Lucy Locket. They went on doing so for a long time.

On leaving the station Germain arranged with the guide to meet that evening at the inn where they were all to spend the night, and wandered off into the temple gardens alone with Keiko. She drank from every fountain, pulled all the prayer bells, bowed to the harnessed horse which awaited the god its master in a stable of precious wood, burned countless sticks of incense and threw coins into all the alms boxes. Seeing her gravity increase as the day went on, he told her: "Come into the forest. There are too many gods here, they're making you sad."

"They'll make me far sadder if I don't bow to them all, for those I leave out will never forgive me."

There are myriads of Shinto *kami* and dozens of Buddhist gods. The unfortunate Westerner who, in his ignorance, takes his girl for a walk through temple gardens will find love's labors lost. The *kami* are watching him.

About two o'clock in the afternoon, hunger drove them into

99

one of the forest glades. They sat down at the foot of a great tree and opened their tins of rice. The rice was cold and clammy; they ate in silence. At last she smiled at him and quoted the old Japanese proverb: "Call nothing splendid till you have seen Nikko."

"Gilles San," she said sweetly, "it is good of you to give up your precious time to me. This is the finest day of my life."

She drew nearer to him. He thought the time ripe for kissing her and slid an arm around her waist.

"Oh no," she said, starting back. "Over there . . . *kami!*"

"What *kami*? Where?"

"That tree behind you."

She pointed to an old knotty pine, almost uprooted. Hundreds of twisted scraps of paper hung from its branches, betokening the prayers and wishes of visitors who reverenced the *kami* of the forest. Germain glanced at the tree, and murmured an ironic prayer to the alien god.

Then they walked for a long while under the enormous vaulted avenues of cryptomerias, almost deserted since this was a weekday. An oppressive green light filtered through the thick foliage, like the colored beams that slant through cathedral windows. They walked without speaking, impressed by the silent majesty of those triumphal avenues through which three centuries earlier had passed the funeral procession of Yayasu Tokugawa, led by his son, the second shogun of that name. When they reached the famous curved bridge that spans the torrent of Daiyu-Gawa they halted.

"*Mihashi!*" Keiko breathed its name with wonder.

Germain looked at the bridge attentively, as if nothing else existed. Knowing with what careful concentration the Japanese gaze at works of art, he was afraid of disappointing the girl if he told her, like an honest Frenchman, that today she was the only object of his admiration. He had seen too many photographs of this bridge, prototype of all *japonaiseries*; it seemed to him rather small, though admirably proportioned. Ten minutes elapsed. He was beginning to grow impatient when, once again, the Japanese miracle worked. It was now his turn to grow ecstatic, as if this bridge with its crimson lacquer and its rich gold fittings had become the sole object and the supreme reward of his journey. His soul soothed by the presence of this masterpiece, he was scarcely aware how typically Japanese was his attitude. In particular, the eloquent stillness of the girl by his side had gently led him to this unusual state of grace. But he understood, too, that in this land of violent contrasts, of squalor and beauty, of grace and vulgarity, a receptive frame of mind was only to be attained through long preludes such as this. If I'm going to visit Japan in this way, he mused, I'm here for the rest of my days! Many other foreigners had made this reflection before him; some had come for a month and stayed for a lifetime.

He noticed that the girl was watching him.

"It's marvelous," he said simply.

She smiled, and the red bridge in its setting of greenery once again became foreign to him. She was so enchanting, so utterly graceful that he called himself every sort of a fool as he imagined the supple body hidden under the cherry-red kimono patterned with large white flowers. And all the way back he talked incessantly. She seemed not to be listening; her face was grave, absorbed in a distant dream. "That bridge," he told himself, "that damned forest and all those ridiculous *kami,* if I'd ever imagined! . . ." He used every known gambit from the subtlest to the most obvious, tried to talk to her about herself with guessing games, invoked the fate which had brought them together: "Don't you think it's strange that you and I, this afternoon . . ."—all in vain.

She answered monosyllabically or not at all. When they were within a hundred yards of the inn he gave it up, cursing Asiatics for their ignorance of the rules of the game. As he fell silent she said to him with great gravity, "You have gone to much trouble to entertain me. I am deeply grateful to you."

This was the last straw! But suddenly, averting her eyes, she added, "Gilles San, I should like to ask you one question. . . . The other day, in front of the inn, in Tokyo, you told me you loved me. Did you mean it?"

He stopped short.

"Beware of Japanese women when they're in love," a French friend had warned him after a long stay in Japan, "or you're done for. They're capable of anything. I knew a naval officer who had a girl friend in Tokyo. He used to stay with her on every trip. Then his company transferred him to the American line, where he served for two years and forgot his Japanese girl. This poor chap lived at Concarneau. He was a pious Breton, a married man with a family. One fine day when he was on leave there came a ring at the door. His wife opened it. There stood the Japanese girl in her best kimono, with a crowd of fascinated onlookers. They're still talking about it at Concarneau. The wretched girl had saved up her pennies for two whole years to buy a third-class ticket, and arrived at Concarneau without knowing a word of French." ("But she was crazy," Germain had said.) "Not crazy, merely faithful. He had told her he loved her, and perhaps he really had loved her. . . ."

"You're not saying anything, Gilles San, have you forgotten already?"

This fresh question enabled him to dodge the first. Oh no, he had not forgotten, he could never forget! He described the scene, the time, the kimono she had worn, even the color of her obi, trying to prove to her that his vivid memory of these details was in itself sufficient reply. But as for the words "Yes, I love you," he no longer dared utter them. Usually he kept them for the women he did not love. And if he said them, how would she react a fortnight later when he had to leave her?

She gazed at him intently for a moment, but he could not fathom the expression in her black eyes. Then, in a musical voice, she made a polite little speech in her own language about the great honor he had done her by accompanying her on her walk, and with a slight bow hurried back to the hotel.

When he met her again in the hall, she was talking to the manager, a distinguished-looking old lady. They held a long conversation with such consistent courtesy in their voices and so many forced smiles that Germain knew something was wrong.

"What's happening, what does the woman want?"

"They're changing my room," the girl replied in a neutral tone. "I cannot explain here. Everybody is watching us. Will you let me come into your room for a few minutes?"

This request did not sound like an encouragement, far from it. He could sense, in the atmosphere around him, an intangible hostility. As soon as she had knelt down, as usual, to close the *shoji* in his bedroom, instead of standing up and returning to the middle of the room she stayed motionless, her hands on her knees, her eyes half-closed as if the thread of her actions had snapped.

"Keiko San, what is the matter, tell me?"

The manager came in, officious and smiling, her white *tabi* gliding silently over the gilded mat. She laid two cups on the low table, two exquisite cups of bluish china incrusted with grains of rice, and with many airs and graces poured out that green, unsweetened tea the mere scent of which recalls Japan. He felt bound to thank her.

"How very charming of that woman to wait on us herself," he said.

"You don't understand the first thing about Japan, Gilles San," Keiko replied as soon as the other woman had gone out. "For one thing I asked for the tea myself, otherwise I should have had no business in your room. And the second thing, do not imagine that she came herself out of kindness, but in order to keep watch on us. At this very moment the whole hotel knows that I am with you, and as soon as I leave your room everybody will be told about it. So I can only stay a very short time."

They knelt down at the table. A maid came in and with long steel rods laid three incandescent lumps of charcoal on the sand in the stove, forming a perfect triangle; then with the tips of her rods she raked the sand in concentric circles, as carefully as the Zen monks of Kyoto tending their esoteric garden. It gave out no heat, but its esthetic value was undeniable.

When he urged Keiko to explain things, she replied in a steady tone that the incident was quite unimportant. Then she began to cry gently. He took her in his arms, clumsily, since it is difficult to do so in a kneeling posture.

"Leave me alone, please leave me alone! If somebody comes in they'll all know that I'm a *pom-pom*."

He was appalled. So that explained the atmosphere of constraint in the hotel! A *pom-pom*! He was familiar with the term, applied as a mark of infamy to low-class women kept by American soldiers.

"But that's absurd, Keiko San! Nobody can think that. For one thing there's no reason. And then I'm neither an American nor a soldier. And besides, you must realize that one's only got to look at you . . ."

He was stumbling over his words. It was too fantastic. He had been advised to choose some little shopgirl who would love him for a month without any complications. When the time came to say good-by he'd give her a present and a purely conventional promise, and then after a few tears, soon dried, it would all be over quite simply. There are thousands of such girls, discreet and pretty and often intelligent, in a country where semi-prostitution is virtually a national vocation. Far from doing so, he had fallen in love with a general's daughter, brought up in an atmosphere where principles were treated seriously. He really was in love with her; at that very moment, he was certain of it.

"You are not an American, but you are a foreigner; for most Japanese that comes to the same thing. Everybody here knows that you are my employer, and that we've been together the whole afternoon, walking alone in the forest. When I arrived, I introduced myself as your colleague. I was given a pretty room. After our walk the manager saw that I was not a real colleague. So she informed me that my room was not available, that she was very sorry but that she'd have to ask me to change to another. The other room is mean and ugly, quite unworthy of this hotel. It must be used for the servants. It's obviously good enough for a *pom-pom*," she paused, "since they assume that I'm not going to sleep in it."

"Shall I send for the manager and insist on her giving you back your room?"

"I should get it back, undoubtedly, with profuse and impressive apologies, and people would think that I am a very expensive *pom-pom* and that you must be very rich. I'd rather it went no further. And now please excuse me, I must leave you."

They rose. She crossed the room and knelt before the *shoji* to open them.

"Keiko San, just now you asked me a question which I did not answer. Do you remember?"

She nodded silently.

"Do you still want to know the answer?"

She nodded again.

"I love you very much."

Still kneeling, she opened the *shoji* which slid back noiselessly in its oiled groove, turned to make a deep ceremonious bow to Germain with her hands laid, finger tips touching, on the mat, then rose and left the room without looking back.

And where has that got me? he thought. He felt wildly happy.

The *shoji* opened again, jerkily pushed aside by a hand that was surely not Japanese. Liliane Laage came in.

"Excuse me for bursting in without warning you, but one can't knock on these wretched doors without thrusting one's arm through them. And so I've made a proper Japanese entry. Still, it's all right, since you're presentable."

She stood tugging at the *shoji* which stubbornly refused to shut.

"These are fiendish contraptions. It always takes me a good hour to get the better of them, if I don't want to break their hinges."

"Unless you tackle them kneeling, you'll only succeed in pushing them off the track. You have to live on your knees in a Japanese house; if you don't keep to that rule you're in for a nervous breakdown."

She squatted, pushed the *shoji* which slid into place unresisting, and asked, "And now tell me, since you've turned Japanese, what am I to do?"

"Lots of complicated things. Just come and sit down, if one can call it that, at this table. Would you like some tea?"

"You too! This is absolutely crazy! Everybody chases after me in this hotel with teapots and teacups, even into my bedroom. Instead of giving me tea, you've got to help me. The manager has just been holding forth to me at great length without supposing for one instant that I could understand her. As usual I said yes. My line, in this country, is to say yes to everything and see what happens. She came back soon after with a teapot and two cups; apparently I'd invited somebody. And then I found myself having tea with *Sensei* Asaki, our neighbor from Tokyo. I wonder how on earth he'd discovered that I was here?"

"A typically Japanese phenomenon! You must realize that nobody who's in any way connected with you can fail to be informed about the least of your actions. Hour by hour, everyone knows where you are and what you're doing, and tells whoever happens to be listening. This sort of petty spying is a Japanese mania and you cannot escape from it. I believe you know this Asaki?"

Germain knew the whole story, which Keiko had lost no time in telling him. He gathered that the *karate* champion had not found favor in the eyes of this highly sensual lady.

"Yes, I know him. But I've no desire to see him, he doesn't amuse me. How can I tell him so politely?" She began to laugh. "Poor man, four hours' train trip for the sake of a cup of tea!"

"Keiko San will fix that . . . I mentioned the Japanese spying mania just now. Would you like proof of it?"

He clapped his hands and called out: "Odjo San, miss!" Three seconds later the door opened to admit the manager.

"There you are! Three seconds to answer, two steps a second, the honorable harridan must have been hiding about three yards away. I had called the maid, but apparently people as important as you and I require the surveillance of the manager in person. *Dozo,*" he said, "Miyamoto San, Miyamoto Keiko . . ."

She dashed to the house telephone which stood on the mat in one corner of the room. Kneeling before it, she seemed to be worshiping the Holy Telephone, the most powerful of Japanese *kami.*

"*Mochi, mochi!*" she began. "*Anone . . .*"

"There she goes," said Germain. "Now be patient, we've at least ten minutes to wait before she's finished her explanations. I don't understand what she's saying, but I'm willing to bet that she's going over the whole story, which you can be sure she knows inside out, beginning with our arrival in Tokyo."

She was still talking when Keiko San came in. Liliane tried to explain, not too bluntly, her wish to get rid of the *karate* champion with all due decorum. The manager, her eyes bulging, her features distorted by the superhuman effort she was making to understand this unfamiliar language, even forgot to smile. Keiko seemed quite self-possessed.

"It's not easy," she replied after a moment's thought. "You're likely to make an enemy of him. *Sensei* Asaki has come to Nikko on business. Hearing by chance of your presence here, he has sought the honor of calling on you . . ."

And as Liliane was obdurate . . .

"I'll tell him, then, that you are touched and delighted by his visit, but that to your great regret a sudden indisposition prevents you from receiving him again."

"She's making a fool of me," was Liliane's reaction as she heard this unconvincing tale. She did not realize that in Japan the requirements of decorum take priority over truth.

"All the same, I'm afraid he's likely to become your enemy," said Keiko San. She was almost out of the room when she turned back with a charming smile to add: "And mine, too."

Sensei Asaki received his answer with such protestations of gratitude that the girl was terrified. He took the last train back to Tokyo, brooding over his vengeance, armed with a stock of information collected from the manager which would enable him to do effective harm. Cecil Brownley traveled back by the same train, unable to bear the prospect of a night without Tomoko San—Miss Prudence—the maid at the Pine Wind Inn.

A quarter of an hour before dinner the telephone rang in Germain's room.

"Hello," said a voice in French. "This is X speaking, secretary at the French Embassy. Are you Monsieur Gilles Germain? Very good. I've got with me in my office Monsieur Miyamoto, your assistant, so I understand"—Germain smiled at hearing this formal description—"who has just informed me of a somewhat unpleasant adventure that has happened to one of your tourists, General de Lure. He was knocked down in a demonstration— No, nothing serious, he's gone back to the hotel, there's nothing to worry about in that respect. But in your absence Monsieur Miyamoto thought it right to inform me, and I have congratulated him on it"—Germain pictured the ecstatic expression on little Miyamoto's face—"particularly as he has quite rightly pointed out that the dignity of the French army, to quote his own words"—This secretary's pulling my leg!—"demands an immediate and vehement protest from our Embassy. A matter of face, you understand. As it seems to me unlikely that General de Lure had any intention of demonstrating his hostility toward the military policy of the United States, I have made a strong but tactful protest to the Imperial Police." (If Germain had had any doubts about the diplomatic qualifications of the speaker, this phrase alone would have sufficed to allay them.) "As a general is involved, the Chief of the Aliens Branch of the Police, Sato San, will come in person next Friday to present his apologies to you. It would be well if you could be there yourself, so as to tell this officer how much you regret his having to spend some minutes of his valuable time on such a visit. You know the style, I don't have to tell you. Sato San is a delightful man moreover, and highly intelligent in spite of appearances. We apologize to one another with great regularity. Can I count on you, then?

Call me one of these days, I must have one or two lunch dates free at the end of the month and I'd be delighted to make your acquaintance. . . ."

At the reception desk the switchboard girl promptly informed the manager. The French Embassy was talking to the honorable foreigner on the first floor. The French Embassy! *So deska!* Aaaa! Aaaa! Aaaaaah! A wave of emotion swept over the group of maids. What an honor for the house! The manager trotted off to Keiko San's room; a mistake, a deplorable mistake . . . it was tomorrow and not today that the room was reserved. If Miss Miyamoto would consent to move back, the manager would take it as a personal favor. She could not bear to think of the honorable foreigner's colleague remaining one moment longer in a room which was quite unworthy of her lofty condition.

Keiko San said no. The manager hurried out, on the verge of irrepressible tears. She rushed into her room and, prostrate on the floor, yielded to convulsive sobs. The whole hotel could hear her. She had lost face.

The tourists gathered for a quick meal in the large ground-floor room. The manager was still invisible, but she had delegated the elite of her staff and sent her choicest dinner service. Keiko San said little and was the first to disappear. Everyone went to bed early, sated with temples and forests.

Germain walked outside the hotel for a few minutes smoking a cigarette, then went back to his room. The *futon,* the carafe and glass, the well-raked stove, the bedside lamp—a paper globe on a delicate bamboo framework—the night-kimono, were all neatly arranged. From a dark corner of the room a voice spoke to him:

"I hope you do not mind. I sent away the maid."

Keiko San was waiting for him, on her knees, motionless, her exquisite hands folded in her lap.

"Do not say anything, Gilles San. You spoke to me earlier. You must not add a word this evening . . . No, no, don't move! Let me keep the illusion that I am choosing my own path."

109

She rose gracefully and unfastened the cord that held her obi in place. He whispered, "Keiko, Keiko San . . . your reputation . . ."

"It is lost already, as you have seen. And besides, what does it matter? If you knew how little I cared! Because this evening, I love you, too."

Two kimonos, one cherry-red with white flowers, the other white patterned in pale pink, fell to her feet like petals. She stood naked, the light from the paper lantern shining dimly on her ivory body with its slender shoulders and round high breasts, and for a moment she hesitated. A tall man, the soothsayer had foretold, who would bring her happiness or grief. . . .

Then she ran to fling herself in his arms.

Thursday

At six P.M. Mme. Tanako, owner of a famous teahouse in Akasaka, escorted by three deferential assistants, inspected the huge room which was waiting to welcome the honorable American and his twenty-five geishas. Long tables of red and gold lacquer had been placed along the sides of the room in a vast horseshoe. In the *tokonoma* alcove, an antique vase held a flower piece consisting of a bough of mossy wood, two long-stemmed flowers and three smooth green leaves. The three deferential assistants greeted the work of art with sonorous, repeated sighs— Mme. Tanako had really surpassed herself!

In the kitchens, the preparations were almost complete. Thirty little blue saucers set out on a table each contained three bamboo shoots. Mme. Tanako took up a saucer and with a practiced finger rearranged the three bamboo shoots in a more perfect harmony with the pattern on the porcelain, and ordered the kitchen maids to imitate her. On other dolls' plates were delicate raw fillets of dory, of a transparent milky whiteness. On the corner of the stove a hundred flasks of the best sake were warming gently. The American won't appreciate this, thought Mme. Tanako, "his giving a party for twenty-five geishas at once proves his ignorance, but the presence of those twenty-five ladies is a challenge to the reputation of my teahouse. All Akasaka will be talking about it."

A maid informed her that a certain Mr. Sato wished to see her. On the visiting card, held vertically, she read: *Chief of the Aliens Branch of the Tokyo Police*. Sato San, the all-powerful Sato San, the protector of Miss Morning Mist! She flew to welcome him.

From their conversation there gradually emerged a request from the policeman, so affably formulated as to admit no refusal. Sato San, dreading unforeseen reactions from the honorable American—one must make allowances for foreigners who are unacquainted with our ways—was anxious to forestall any untoward incident by keeping a discreet watch from a neighboring room over the remarkable dinner party organized by Mme. Tanako. The latter bowed and led him into a small private room, separated from the large room by a door of gray parchment. From this lookout post you could hear everything. Mme. Tanako herself frequently made use of it. If the honorable Sato San was afraid of being bored during this tedious dinner, Mme. Tanako would be delighted to send pretty Morning Mist to keep him company.

Sato San refused. His girl friend understood English and he had planned an important role for her. He merely suggested that Mme. Tanako put her on the left hand of the American in case he spoke too low for Sato to catch his words.

Realizing the importance of neutralizing so formidable a spectator, Mme. Tanako insisted that the honorable policeman must not be left alone. "It would be difficult for me to wait on you myself," she said. "I assure you I most deeply regret it, but running this dinner is going to take up all my time. So I'll send you Harumi San, a *maiko* from my house, a very young girl."

Very young, presumably a virgin. Sato's eyelids narrowed. Mme. Tanako heaved a sigh. Harumi San was sixteen. She had bought her four years earlier from a Kyushu fisherman who had been glad to sell his youngest daughter in order to pay his debts. Mme. Tanako owned a flourishing teahouse but did not regularly deal in geishas, just as one may possess a single horse without owning a stable. Thus Mme. Tanako speculated on her *maiko*, not from greed but as a matter of policy. Virgin *maikos* are usually kept for rich clients as a special honor. Until now Mme. Tanako had preserved Harumi San's virtue for a powerful industrialist from Yokohama whose patronage she hoped to win. Alas, she would have to sacrifice the favors of the industrialist. With a million-yen dinner in half an hour's time, those of Sato San seemed more urgent. If all went well, she'd send for Harumi San as soon as the party ended. If not . . . well, the girl would have to stay.

The first stages of the meal went smoothly. Somewhat surprised to find that there were twenty-five of them for only a couple of men, the geishas soon made the best of it. After all it was easy money, they decided. Douglas Cadwallader IV, seated in the place of honor with Miss Cloudless Sky on his right hand and Miss Morning Mist on his left, seemed determined to avoid blunders. He behaved with perfect courtesy, tirelessly exchanging with his neighbors countless cups of sake previously dipped, as etiquette requires, in a bowl of tepid water. Unflinching, he swallowed everything that was offered him, dried tunnyfish, chrysanthemum leaves, raw dory or sea lichen. From time to time he winked at Miyamoto. The latter looked supremely happy. Seated between his cousin Miss Cloudless Sky and a delicious creature called Spring Snow, he fancied himself back in the days of his father the general. Kneeling behind him, somewhat in the background, Mme. Tanako kept watch. Another hour and Harumi San would be saved, saved for the industrialist.

Sato San, in his hide-out, drank cup after cup of sake, meanwhile plying his young companion with liquor. She was getting slightly tipsy, and if the evening ended as he had foreseen he would have a willing *maiko* at his disposal. Mme. Tanako came to tell him that a photographer from the *Asahi*, that important daily, wanted to take a few pictures.

"Let him come," said the policeman, "the American will not mind. In his country one will do anything for a photograph."

In fact Sato San had himself sent for the photographer, whose presence would enable him to score points in a ticklish dispute in which he was engaged with the all-powerful U. S. Embassy.

After his twentieth cup of sake Cadwallader discovered that his right-hand neighbor was adorable. The long sleeves of her kimono fell back gracefully to disclose her pretty, round bare arms. As they exchanged cups he took hold of her wrist, and found it smooth and cool. Their knees were touching. He suddenly became aware of this, and shuddered with indignation as he pictured that fragile body a prey to debauchery.

"She is very beautiful!" said Miyamoto to please him.

"Too beautiful for her job," he muttered between clenched teeth.

He must act, to save her and others like her. He rose slowly to his feet, saying over in his mind the words of the short speech he had prepared. The explosion of the photographer's flashbulb took him by surprise, but he reacted with a broad grin that showed his dazzling teeth and bespoke his radiant health and optimism.

Three shrill notes on the samisen drowned the first words of his sentence. Mme. Tanako, fearful of the potential peril implied by the presence of Sato San, had taken no chances on seeing him rise to his feet and had given the signal for dancing. Cadwallader sank back on his knees. Miss Morning Mist flew off to tell Sato San: "He said Dear Sisters . . ."

Mme. Tanako awaited her orders.

"It is all right," said the policeman, "next time let him speak, he can only talk nonsense, so let him talk nonsense."

Harumi San, lightheaded and bright-eyed, quite unconscious of what was going on around her, was roaring with laughter. Mme. Tanako gazed at her reproachfully.

Douglas tossed off five bowls of sake, slyly pressed on him by Miss Morning Mist, back at her post. "The more he drinks the more nonsense he will talk," Sato San had pointed out. Miss Cloudless Sky, surrounded by six other geishas, performed the dance of the Shikoku fishermen. Her movements were formal and yet flexible; her body assumed unexpected attitudes. There was a lull in which everyone unreservedly admired that mysterious choreography which only the Japanese can fully appreciate. Sato San himself watched through the half-open door of his alcove, and did not miss a single step of the dance. The American applauded vigorously, then raised both hands in the air to show that he was about to speak. Sato San smiled. Miss Morning Mist prepared to listen carefully. The reporter, who knew English, got out his notebook and fountain pen. Mme. Tanako hung her head, feeling the cold blast of defeat.

"Dear sisters . . ." began Cadwallader. ("You translate," he whispered to Miyamoto, "I won't be long-winded.") "Dear sisters, it's been a great pleasure for me to see your games and dances, your lovely kimonos, in the wonderful setting of this teahouse, all so typical of your old Japanese civilization, and I'd like to thank you for answering my appeal in such large numbers."

He paused. Mr. Miyamoto, who was prepared for the speech but not for its contents, interpreted. The exordium surprised him, but seemed suitably flattering. The young ladies were pleased with their compliments, although the term "dear sisters" puzzled them slightly. Nobody, obviously, had ever considered them as sisters before. Quite spontaneously they all began to chuckle softly, putting their hands in front of their mouths. Satisfied with what he took to be a murmur of approbation the American went on:

"I have called you sisters because on this earth of ours all men and all women, whatever their race and their religion, form part of the same family, the great human family! That's why we all have to help one another."

Mr. Miyamoto, feeling slightly uneasy, began to betray him. Having been taken unawares, he alluded in vague terms to the great human family, but passed over in silence any suggestion of brotherly relations between the American and the geishas. The exact words of the speech, however, were inexorably set down in the journalist's notebook. Sato San, inured to the difficulties of the English language, felt a blissful satisfaction pervade him.

"And that is why," Douglas went on, "the Anti-Slavery League of the Sons of the American Revolution, of which I am President, has sent me to try to help you. We know the difficulties of your life, we know the state of subjection—" He hesitated, but as he had been drinking he was not afraid of words, "almost of slavery in which you are kept against your will. In the name of democracy, in the name of the United States, land of freedom, I proclaim to you: The day of your deliverance is at hand!"

Miyamoto, aghast, opened his mouth to speak: no sound came out.

"Well, what are you waiting for?" said Douglas.

"I can't go on, sir," he managed to stammer. How had he floundered into such a situation?

"I can't go on," he said, "I didn't understand very well."

"That's all right," said Cadwallader, "I'll repeat it. . . . And I proclaim to you: The day of your deliverance is at hand."

The astonished journalist had stopped writing; he took this opportunity to catch up. Miss Morning Mist, who had also understood the speech, broke into strident laughter. Twenty-four geishas followed her example with a chorus of giggles.

"There's nothing funny about that," said the American. "What's come over them?"

"It's the custom in Japan," said Miyamoto, at his wit's end.

Sato San congratulated himself on having come. For the past few months the Japanese government, influenced by certain left-wingers and by the American-controlled Protestant Leagues, had forbidden the purchase of little girls by geisha houses. The mistresses of these *geishaya* circumvented the law by calling the purchase price "an advance on wages," and in this they had the support of a large section of Japanese public opinion, which considered the geisha business essential for the maintenance of old traditions. This was Sato San's opinion too. He was a traditionalist, like so many Japanese. If the geishas were suppressed, the teahouses would disappear too. There would be an end to those dinner parties, dances, kimonos . . . and charming women. No Japanese could envisage such a state of affairs.

"Yes or no," said Douglas, "are you going to translate?"

"Right away, sir, right away . . . The honorable Mr. Cadwallader," he went on in Japanese, "asks me to tell you that thanks to you he has enjoyed the most wonderful day in his life."

Miyamoto had betrayed him. For he, too, approved of the existence of geishas, and no one was going to make him alter his opinion. "That young fellow's no fool," noted Sato San. "We will see about finding him some useful job."

"Finished already?" asked Douglas in astonishment.

"Japanese is a very concise language!"

"Then I'll go on: The Sons of the American Revolution has therefore decided to award a considerable grant to any geisha who is willing to redeem herself in order to live a life worthy of a free woman. Don't hesitate, come and see me at the Pine Wind Inn. Together we will draw up your dossier, which will be submitted for approval to the Managing Committee of the League in New York . . ."

He added in a tone of great earnestness: "We shall not desert you!"

"Mr. Cadwallader's dearest wish," translated Miyamoto, "is to meet you all again in the near future."

He stopped, exhausted, his mind a blank, but with a sense of having averted disaster. Mme. Tanako, dimly realizing the urgent need for a diversion, clapped her hands. The geishas meekly followed suit, but they had not failed to notice Miyamoto's embarrassment. Something dreadful had been happening, to judge by the expression on the face of the honorable interpreter. They'd soon find out. News spreads fast in Akasaka. Eager to exchange their impressions with their Mama Sans they hurried out one after the other and disappeared in a whirl of taxis, while Cadwallader beamed good-by at the teahouse door. Miss Cloudless Sky was the last to leave. He gazed after her, his heart throbbing with an unfamiliar excitement.

"I shall stay behind to verify the bill," said Miyamoto. He could not face another minute of the American's presence.

"O.K., I'll be seeing you tomorrow."

Feeling the need for a walk, the apostle of the geishas strode off rapidly and vanished around the street corner. Freed from his nightmare at last, Miyamoto hurried back into the teahouse. It was essential to have a word with Mme. Tanako. He found her in the main room, together with Miss Morning Mist, the journalist, and an important-looking person whom he did not know. Mme. Tanako introduced Sato San. Sato San, the Chief of Police, who was to come to apologize to General de Lure! Miyamoto shivered; for one thing, because of the combination of respect and dread with which the Japanese regard their police, and for another because it is better to have a clear conscience when so important a personage is going to eat humble pie. Miyamoto was in a vulnerable spot.

Sato San made exactly the same reflections.

"One day soon," he said to Miyamoto, "I shall ask you to be kind enough to come and see me at Police Headquarters. Until then, and especially during my call tomorrow, not a word about what has taken place here! The honorable American must remain in ignorance of my presence in this room, and if anyone else puts questions to you, please confine yourself to your very skillful translation. This may be a serious matter involving the honor of Japan."

With the deepest of bows, Miyamoto slunk away.

"As for you," said Sato San to the journalist, "remember our agreement. I sent for you myself to this dinner, promising you the chance of a sensational report. I did not mislead you. This story will make the Americans lose face and seem utterly ridiculous. But the time is not yet ripe. As we agreed, you will write your article and submit a copy of it to me as soon as possible, with prints of your photographs. But you will await my permission to publish. If a single line about this evening's events appears against my will I shall be obliged to speak about it to your editor. This is no mere personal whim," he added more gently. "You know that the United States Embassy is determined to bring before an American court the case of the G.I., Marshall, who murdered a Japanese girl. A similar case occurred last year and the criminal was acquitted. For these people the life of a Japanese is as cheap as a dog's. Thanks to your article I shall force them to alter their decision, or else I shall hold them up to public ridicule. Such are my reasons, and I am glad to see that you appreciate them. Let me have the article tomorrow morning."

The journalist promised, vowed, asserted his loyalty, bowed very low and left the teahouse, proud at having a part to play in so delicate a game. Indeed, the honorable Sato San need have made no threats; the journalist came from Hiroshima, and he remembered.

Sato San turned to Miss Morning Mist: "Will you translate the American's speech for Mme. Tanako without altering a word of it?"

This geisha, too, had been bought as a child. The insignificant peasant girl from a tiny Hondo village had become one of the most famous geishas in Tokyo. She was proud of her position, for she was received by the most important people in the capital and even played a not inconsiderable role in political life. To be publicly dubbed a prostitute by a mannerless barbarian was something she could not tolerate nor, indeed, understand. Each country has its own moral code—in Japan, that of the Christians is the least acceptable and the most useless of imports.

She translated Cadwallader's proposals into Japanese. Mme. Tanako nearly fainted. If the neighborhood heard of such appalling suggestions, her house would be dishonored. No geisha would ever consent to be entertained there. Her fortune and her fate lay in the hands of Sato San. A single word from him, and ruin would overwhelm poor Tanako. The policeman, massive and inscrutable, watched her panic.

"If the honorable Sato San would consent to stay a little longer, my house is at his disposal. He will naturally appreciate that after so important a dinner my presence is urgently required in the kitchen."

She left the hall with her eyes cast down, showing no sign of feeling, casting no glance toward that inner room where little Harumi San lay in a tipsy stupor. Sato San opened the door. The *maiko* lay supine on the mat, her eyes half-closed. Unconscious she looked even younger than she was. Her white-powdered face was like a doll's.

"Undress her," he ordered Miss Morning Mist.

His eyes were invisible between closed lids. Flasks of sake had been left on the low table; he shook them one after the other before he found a full one, which he tossed off in one gulp. The *maiko* was naked: a childish, flat-bosomed body.

There was a great scream.

Mme. Tanako, hiding in her kitchen, started.

The *maiko* screamed for the second time.

In every police force in the world, somebody takes advantage of professional opportunities. . . .

Friday

At about ten o'clock in the morning, a special messenger brought Sato San the article and the photographs. The headline proclaimed: LATEST AMERICAN INSULT and the subhead ran: *During Sumptuous Feast, Rich American Calls Twenty-five Geishas Prostitutes.* For once the *Asahi*, usually so moderate, did not mince its words. Sato San suspected the editor of currying favor with him, which he could quite safely do since the article would probably never be published. Moreover its bitterness seemed quite plausible, even from the prudent *Asahi*. As a result of the demonstrations against American bases, and particularly of the Marshall murder case, Japanese opinion had become increasingly hostile toward the United States. And surely it is the duty of a great newspaper to follow public opinion. The article concluded:

Now, when American courts are preparing, in a travesty of justice, to acquit the murderer of a Japanese woman, it ill becomes the land of call girls to offer us a lesson in morality.

Armed with these documents, Sato San paid a call on the Political Adviser to the U. S. Embassy. On highly urgent business, he specified. By eleven o'clock he was in the diplomatic sanctum.

"Dear Mr. Sato," said the Political Adviser, "I am so glad to see you. I wanted to tell you that our resident American citizens here are worried about certain displays of hostility from which some of them have recently suffered. To be sure nothing very serious has occurred—a car window smashed, a few insulting words and regrettable gestures, nothing that can affect the friendly relations between our two countries. We are well aware that these are isolated incidents due in most cases to undesirables. Nevertheless the Embassy is afraid lest these incidents, exaggerated by the American press, may have an adverse effect on the Congressional vote on fresh credits to be granted your country. As Chief of the Aliens Branch you must have been aware of these happenings." Then he added in a more familiar tone: "Tell me frankly, as a friend, what's your opinion about them?"

Sato San observed to himself that every American he had come across had immediately proclaimed himself his friend. He pretended to be deep in thought.

"Frankly, since you ask me, I am somewhat anxious. Police reports suggest a state of tension. I think it would all quickly subside if the soldier Marshall were handed over to a Japanese court."

The Adviser sighed: "I know, I know! You're quite right! But the law's the law. Any American soldier, in whatever country he is arrested, must be judged by a United States court. The Ambassador is being inundated with cables reminding him of this law: seven Senators, twenty-five Representatives, a Governor, and four leading newspapers have intervened, not to mention the Association of American Mothers." He gave a weary smile. "And believe me, American mothers are not to be trifled with."

"I understand," said Sato San, "but this decision is nonetheless prejudicial to the good relations existing between our two countries. Particularly," he feigned hesitancy, "as a fresh motive of tension has recently been communicated to me. Hitherto I have succeeded in preventing its diffusion, but my influence is so slight . . ."

His eyes cast down, his face calm and gentle, he looked like a fat Buddha.

"What now?" asked the diplomat quickly.

Sato San drew the *Asahi* article from his pocket and placed it on the desk without a word. A plot, a cunning plot, the American concluded after scanning the text.

"Please excuse me a moment," he said to Sato San, and went out with the article in his hand.

Cadwallader, summoned to the telephone, confirmed his words and asserted his intention of continuing his efforts. The Adviser refrained from calling him an idiot; such terms are not used toward the President of the powerful Sons of the American Revolution, which controls seventy daily papers and sixteen weeklies, not to mention thousands of committees. The harm was done now, he could only hope to restrict its damaging effects. The Ambassador, urgently consulted, informed him that a recent order from the United States directed him to hand over the soldier Marshall to Japanese justice, but that he might, if he saw fit, use this concession (an unpopular one in America) to press for the settlement of certain outstanding questions.

"This geisha business may put us in a bad light," he told the Adviser. "It's up to you to impress on Sato that I am quite prepared to use my influence in the Marshall affair, but that in return he must see that this deplorable misunderstanding is buried once and for all, and without any help from us. We can't possibly take action against this Cadwallader. We'd be slaughtered by about eighty newspapers. Get out of it as best you can; I'm counting on you."

The Adviser went back to his office. Sato San listened respectfully to his prudent explanations, then expressed profound gratitude.

"It's most important," the Adviser insisted, "that Mr. Cadwallader never realize that his mission is being obstructed. If that should ever happen, the Ambassador asks me to warn you that in no case could he possibly intervene, but that his decision regarding the Marshall case might then be modified, whatever the consequences."

"You need have no fear," replied Sato San with a smile in his eyes, "Mr. Cadwallader shall carry out his mission, at least he shall believe he is doing so, and nobody shall know anything about it."

"When I think," the Adviser reflected on Sato San's departure, "that this remarkable man only earns thirty thousand yen a month!" (His own salary was in the neighborhood of eight hundred thousand.)

Early that afternoon Sato San crossed the threshold of the Pine Wind Inn. "And now we will take care of the French!"

Gilles Germain, General de Lure and Miyamoto received him in a small parlor. The *shoji* opened on to the garden pool where huge pink and white carp rose gleaming to the surface of the water. Mme. Hashi served tea. The conversation took a simple and friendly turn from the start. General de Lure joked cheerfully about the purple lump on his forehead. And when Sato San suggested punishing the policeman who was responsible for it, he urged him to do nothing of the sort.

"On the other hand," the general said, "I should be glad to know what happened to the crippled soldier whom I saw knocked down close to me. If anyone is to be punished, let it be the man who struck that unfortunate creature."

Miyamoto writhed on his cushion. Since last night's incident he felt like a hunted man; he would have run away from his own shadow. The police officer was expecting this request, for his reports suggested that the foreigner had been struck down while trying to help the beggar. He had made inquiries, suspecting some obscure connection between the cripple and the French general.

"The man left the hospital this morning and was able to go home."

"Can you give me his address?"

"Nothing could be simpler. The superintendent of the Yasukuni district is sure to have it. May I ask, General, why you take such an interest in this beggar?"

"I spent thirty years of my life in the army," the general said, "and I cannot possibly remain unmoved by the misfortunes of a man who is neglected by both public and private authority. His destitute state surprised me all the more when I happened to learn that he was an officer of the Imperial Army, Lieutenant Hakayama. I cannot understand why the Japanese Government grants no pension, provides no assistance for its former officers."

Sato San pensively examined his teacup. Should he, in his turn, express surprise that France should be a rich enough country to grant pensions to its millions of defeated soldiers? He abstained, out of politeness toward this Frenchman who appeared motivated by the best intentions. Could he admit, without leading him to form erroneous conclusions about the honor of Japan and the dignity of its unfortunate warriors, that in his own conquered and humiliated country, where admirals had sunk to petty officers, where colonels were employed as factory porters and generals as clerks at ten thousand yen a month, where the widows of high-ranking officers sold their kimonos one by one in order to subsist, the fate of a mere lieutenant, however distressing, could interest nobody? Should he tell him, finally, that in his overpopulated country where so many able-bodied men struggled in vain to find work, the unfit were irremediably doomed?

"Compared with the other disasters that have overtaken my country," he replied at last, "the fate of her soldiers counts for very little. After all, they were just doing their job. . . . But since you are so kind as to take an interest in this Lieutenant Hakayama, I will give you his address as soon as I have it."

Pity is a feeling unknown in Japan, particularly that paradoxical sort of pity which impels Westerners, in the words of a former Japanese minister, to "shed tears over the fate of one orphan who by some miracle has escaped from the massacre they themselves ordered." It did not worry Sato San that the lieutenant should be forced to beg. But that he should consent to beg—that revolted him, that shocked him to the core. Did the general want to help the mendicant officer? So much the better. Sato San would smooth his path, would even, if need be, order the wretch to let himself be overwhelmed with gifts and good will. May he die of shame, thought the policeman, and may such degradation as his disappear with him forever.

His heavy face assumed so dark an expression that Germain, suddenly remembering the words of the Embassy secretary, thanked him profusely. The general joined in; Sato San replied in kind. They parted on the best of terms. Only Miyamoto retained a slightly uneasy feeling from this visit. As he rose, the policeman said to him in Japanese, "You will be at my office on Monday morning."

As he passed through the gateway of the inn, Sato San caught sight of the cross standing in the garden near the Buddhist temple.

"Miss Simpson, I presume?" he said to Miyamoto, who was escorting him.

Poor Miyamoto felt his legs give way beneath him. Was nothing secret from this terrible man?

Sato San heaved a sigh. "These foreigners," he muttered, "would have done better to stay at home."

Miyamoto went back into the inn, deep in thought; he was seriously wondering whether the policeman had not spoken the truth. . . .

Saturday

Mr. Miyamoto had an appointment at four o'clock that afternoon with *Sensei* Asaki. It was now five minutes to four. Standing under the porch of the inn, Mr. Miyamoto stared at the rain that was sweeping over the garden. He was of two minds. Last Tuesday at the local baths, when he heard the obscene comments about Mme. Laage with which *Sensei* Asaki regaled his friends, he had vowed to demand an apology. But since Tuesday, having been swept against his will into a sea of troubles, he felt his enthusiasm for the West grow cool. He still retained a certain liking, nonetheless, for Liliane Laage, who perfectly embodied his conception of a Frenchwoman, unconventional and unprejudiced. She had not planted any crosses, she was always pleasant to talk to, she appeared quite indifferent to the fate of geishas and beggars and had not yet attracted the dreaded attention of Sato San. Added to which the honorable interpreter never saw her go past without a secret thrill of admiration for that regal bust, sheathed in a close-fitting, brightly colored sweater. He was fascinated by the mystery of the Western female figure. One day while she took her bath at the inn he had gazed undisturbed through the dense steam, and she had not taken the slightest offense. He remembered in vivid detail—such breasts, ample, firm and pointed like the choicest pears, he had never seen in his life before. It was a point in her favor, too, to have given herself to a Japanese; he felt a sort of pride in this, and a secret hope: suppose one day . . . What a story to tell his friends! . . . But wasn't that Asaki's attitude? No, Asaki San had behaved coarsely, which was not surprising from an uncultured athlete whose only accomplishment was breaking bricks. Men of breeding are more reticent about their conquests.

Miyamoto put on high wet-weather *geta,* opened an umbrella of oiled paper and set out under the relentless downpour. His mind was made up. He had ceased to connect Mlle. Laage with the rest of the tourists. He had no intention of defending the West. It was only his pride, hurt by the insults to the desirable Liliane, that drove him to this noble action.

As for *Sensei* Asaki, he had not remained idle. Having called up the Nikko hotel he had learned without surprise that Keiko San had not slept in her room the other night. And so, whereas that Frenchwoman had dismissed him with contempt, a woman of his own race had shamelessly yielded herself to a Frenchman! They'd pay dearly for all this! *Sensei* Asaki was not a tender-hearted creature, and his service in the Japanese shock troops had made him even more callous. A certain small village in the Philippines would still remember him as a savage non-commissioned officer. Years had passed and his brutal instincts had lain dormant; now they were aroused again by resentment, as he brooded with gloomy ferocity on his humiliation. Let him come then, the white men's little flunkey! He'd hear something about his sister, the Frenchman's tart! That would teach him to grovel before his honorable visitors!

As soon as they stood face to face Asaki barked out his phrase of welcome, the shortest he could think of in the vast repertory of polite formulae. Miyamoto sensed his intention, cut short his own preamble and without more ado referred to the scene at the public baths.

Sensei Asaki laughed spitefully. "And you have the face to protest? You should instead be pleased, for the white man deserves nothing but contempt, as you will soon find out if you do not know it already. You are the only Japanese I know to stand up for them! You think so much of the Frenchwoman's honor that you cannot even worry about your own sister's! It's not a song about Liliane San that I should have sung the other day in the *furo* but one about Keiko San, Miyamoto Keiko! Keep your indignation for the Frenchman who pays you, and who, I suppose, pays your sister, too."

Mr. Miyamoto paled. Asaki continued in a low incisive voice: "All white people are alike. I have nothing but contempt for them, and I am helping you to gain your revenge by shaming this Frenchwoman in public. She's playing the lady now, but I had her at my mercy, here on this mat! The lady! I will make her grovel and the whole neighborhood shall know about it! You ought to be grateful to me—after what happened to your sister, you ought to be helping me. We have tolerated the foreigners long enough! They bomb our towns, shame our Emperor and take away our land and now they seek our women. And our Japanese women fall for their talk of sex equality, as you just discovered yourself."

Miyamoto assented in silence. These words revived long dormant memories: his father's desperate suicide, his mother driven mad by the bombardment, their home so completely destroyed that he had failed to find even the street where it had stood, the shortage of rice, the bitter mockery of the candy proffered by khaki-clad soldiers, his own experience with semistarvation, and now his own sister Keiko's denial of the past. . . .

He protested feebly: "All whites are not American. France has done us no harm, and Mlle. Laage is French—"

"So is your sister's lover! And what is France? A small decadent country, America's stooge! There is no difference between any of those people, wherever they go, whoever they are. I have only done my duty as a Japanese, and it is time you remembered your own!"

Miyamoto gave up. He was in no position to answer. Asaki, in secret triumph, watched him go off with bowed back.

The rain had stopped. Indifferent to the dark puddles flooding the pavement, Miyamoto pondered as he walked: should he go to Germain and present his resignation without an explanation? Sato San would never allow that, and the little interpreter knew that he was a key pawn in the policeman's involved game. Should he indignantly forbid Germain to see Keiko again? Only one solution was possible: to send his sister away without delay. Meanwhile, during the fortnight that still remained before the Frenchman's departure, he would obey orders whoever gave them, and wash his hands of the consequences.

In the garden of the inn he met Liliane Laage in slacks and sweater, her hair hanging loose on her shoulders.

"I'm going for a walk," she said, "will you come with me?"

A glorious woman! Her very smile always seemed an invitation.

127

"Excuse me," he said with an effort, "I haven't the time." Then he added almost inaudibly, "Mademoiselle, beware of Asaki San. . . ."

She gave a deep throaty laugh and went on her way. Her full round hips swayed with the rhythm of her steps. Once again he admired her beauty. But his decision allowed no exceptions. Who cared what happened to her? He had given her up like all the rest. He went into the inn.

Germain was waiting for him there, and remarked, "Hello, I've just been looking for you. It's Saturday and we must settle our accounts."

They went into a small parlor. Germain drew a notebook from his pocket.

"Let us see," he said, "I agreed to pay you once a fortnight. Three thousand yen a day, plus a bonus of two thousand, that makes five thousand multiplied by fifteen: I owe you seventy-five thousand yen. First let me tell you how pleased I am with your work; our friends are delighted; Mr. Cadwallader in particular praises you to the skies. But between ourselves," he dropped his voice, "don't think yourself obliged to help him in all his curious projects. He has a mania for crusading, but he's not dangerous. Find him a geisha who'll amuse him for a while, if you can. He'll be quite satisfied and so shall I, and the Agency won't lose a client. But let's return to our accounts . . ."

He held out a voluminous bundle of notes. (The Japanese print no paper money of higher denominations than a thousand yen; it's a matter of practical psychology, since the average working-class wage is ten thousand yen a month.)

Miyamoto took the money and buried it in his pocket. Seventy-five thousand yen! ten times as much as he had ever possessed at one time. The young man was honest but, at the same time, eager for success; he had earned the money fairly, and his present feelings need not prevent him from taking it. As to the next installment, he'd plenty of time to make up his mind, and he could always refuse part, saying that he didn't deserve it. . . .

"I owe your sister some money too. You had asked for two thousand yen a day for her. Here are thirty thousand. Please be kind enough to give them to her."

Germain preferred to keep love and business separate. The young man's eyes narrowed. "She will be very grateful to you," he said. He was choking with resentment.

"Tomorrow of course you are free. We will meet again on Monday."

Germain rose and held out his hand. Miyamoto made an abrupt, deep bow and ran off as if the devil were at his heels. Peculiar fellow! thought the Frenchman. When I bow he offers me his hand, and when I offer my hand he bows. We shall never understand each other!

Mr. Miyamoto rushed through the hall, tore upstairs four steps at a time and tumbled into his sister's room. Keiko San was kneeling in front of a doll-sized dressing table, reading.

"I've brought you your night's wages," he said. "Thirty thousand yen for you, and you've earned them. Not bad pay for a *pom-pom*."

He put down the money on the dressing table and stood waiting for her answer. She shut her book, rose to her feet and faced him quite calmly. Weighing her words, she replied, "I knew you would find out sooner or later. Otherwise I should have told you myself, since you're my brother and the head of the family. But the way you've insulted me entitles me to tell you that although you have the right to know, you have no power over my feelings or actions. Things are not what they were twenty years ago. You forget the war, which men lost through their pride and vanity. Women are free today."

He hit her twice, violently, leaving a mark on her cheek. She remained motionless.

"Our honorable father would have acted as you've done," she said, "even more brutally perhaps. Out of respect for his memory I have allowed you to insult and strike me, for when he lived he would have had the right to do so. He would even have driven me out of his house, he'd have cast me off, maybe cursed me.

Those times are past. Our father has taken his authority with him into his grave, like thousands of other men who died for nothing."

Pale with rage, Miyamoto raised his hand to strike her again. This time she drew back.

"I have been humbly respectful of our traditions, you've no right to expect more of me; I won't stand for it. I shall take orders from you for the last time, because one can't cast off the old ways all at once. I suppose you intend to send me away from here. I'll grant you the right to do so for one fortnight. It will be better so. You shall decide on the place I am to go to. I will obey. After that fortnight I shall come back. The inn will be empty then and your pride will be satisfied. We can go home again. But never again, that I swear to you, shall you impose your will on me. Now I am ready; where am I to go?"

Since her return from Nikko, Keiko San had already determined on self-banishment as an escape from her own weakness. By suggesting it as though in obedience to her brother's orders, she was saving his face. He realized this and hung his head, almost ashamed of his inglorious victory. Oh, how right Asaki had been.

"You must go to our cousin at Okinoshima tonight. Nobody must know where you are nor why you left. Go home and pack your things. You have just time to catch the evening train."

She collected a few articles in a silk handkerchief which she knotted at the corners, bowed to her brother and went out. . . .

Later, Mr. Miyamoto took leave of the Frenchman.

"My sister has been called away suddenly," he said, staring down at the mat. "Our aunt is ill. She begs you to excuse her."

Germain understood, and only asked, "Is it far away?"

"Somewhere in the west."

A typically Japanese reply!

V

Japanese Revenge

That Monday morning, Sato San entered his office on the third floor of the Tokyo Police Headquarters in high spirits. The office was a large one, clean but shabby. A threadbare carpet, two dilapidated armchairs, paint peeling from the walls, all told of the impoverished state of the Japanese administration. Since he often had to receive visitors, he had repeatedly asked for decent furniture, but without success. It would be highly inadvisable, the Chief Commissioner's office had told him, to give an impression of luxury to the foreigners, particularly the Americans, who on returning home would promptly spread the tale that Japan prospered. Moreover, it was pointed out to him, he was the only Departmental Head who could offer his visitors real armchairs.

Having scanned the morning papers while traveling in a crowded bus from his distant suburb, he was feeling well satisfied. Most of the editorial articles welcomed the wise and friendly gesture made by the United States in handing over the Marshall case to Japanese jurisdiction. The official communiqué from the U. S. Embassy merely stated that this decision might have

131

to undergo certain delays in application. Which, being interpreted, meant that the Embassy would not hand over the criminal until the Cadwallader affair had been definitely buried.

Sato San was warmly congratulated by the Chief Commissioner as soon as he arrived. To crown his joy he learned that in consideration of the importance of his work, a car and driver would be set at his disposal for professional journeys, and new furniture provided for his office. Such concrete symbols of dignity serve the same purpose in Japan as do medals and decorations among Western officialdom. When brought up-to-date on the Cadwallader affair, the Chief Commissioner nearly died of laughter.

"It could not be easier," he said. "Treat him like Townsend Harris."

Townsend Harris had been the first American diplomat on Japanese soil, in the nineteenth century. In order to keep him quiet and facilitate surveillance, the Mikado's government had provided him with a geisha. Having fulfilled her mission to the satisfaction of the government, the poor woman received no reward. Her compatriots despised her for having shared a white man's bed. She drowned her sorrow in alcohol and ended her days sadly, in shame and destitution. Puccini immortalized her under the name of Madama Butterfly.

"I thought of that, sir," replied Sato. "The American shall have his geisha without delay. I may add that she will certainly enjoy a happier fate than her unfortunate predecessor."

"I couldn't care less," the Chief Commissioner replied curtly. And the interview was at an end.

Sato San went back to his office. Three problems faced him, very different but all caused by the intolerable penchant of Westerners for interfering in Japanese private life. They'd had hotels built to their own taste in all the major towns, massive blocks of concrete with beds, bathrooms and elevators. And yet, this was not enough to neutralize them. Some of them escaped from their prisons-without-bars and set out to understand Japan with the naïve passion of explorers or missionaries.

The Japanese, who were quite content with their own customs and creeds and not in the least anxious to be understood, found this hard to tolerate. Most of the Westerners were satisfied with a Buddhist service, a *sukiyaki,* and a furtive visit to the restricted district. Others, more tenacious, excitedly ferreted out evidence of grave problems needing the urgent intervention of Western wisdom. It was at this stage that difficulties arose, when the tacit conspiracy of the whole Japanese nation was inadequate to quell the indiscretion of foreigners, and it was here that Sato San brought into play the inexhaustible resources of his ingenuity.

Today three foreigners, each in his own way, menaced Japan's cherished privacy: Miss Simpson, Douglas Cadwallader and General de Lure. In spite of their obvious good will they were, in fact, meddling in matters that did not concern them. It might have been simpler to point out to them the impropriety or absurdity of their efforts. But no Japanese is able or willing to explain himself or his country to foreigners. He can only close up like a clam or show his prickles like a hedgehog. The case of the two Americans, however, called for a certain diplomatic skill. Douglas Cadwallader, in particular, because of his barter value in the Marshall case, could not be attacked direct. According to the verbal agreement reached between Sato San and the U. S. Embassy, he must be allowed to retain the illusion that he had usefully contributed to the moral welfare of the geishas. The policeman considered this problem solved. The attentions lavished by Cadwallader on Miss Cloudless Sky at the dinner party made her an obvious choice for the role of Butterfly. Sato San had sent for her and expected her momentarily. He would merely have to convince her.

Miss Simpson's file showed her to be a rich woman. It was therefore out of the question to keep her quiet merely by police action. The U. S. Embassy would protest all the more strenuously for having had to give way over Cadwallader. Should he have the cross removed secretly by night? The lady, whose obstinate nature was confirmed by all reports, would only plant another the next day, perhaps right in the middle of the temple court. Toyota San, the Prior of the Monastery, would not be content with a telephone call this time, but would bring his family influence into play. A former member of the nobility, connected with the Imperial family, he had only to utter a few words to ruin the policeman's career. Sato San pondered. Since that crazy woman wanted her cross, she'd have to be persuaded to stick it somewhere else, where no important personality could take umbrage. He remembered a small plot of land owned by the police in the neighborhood of the Pine Wind Inn. There had been talk of building a police station there, but the decision had been put off from year to year. Sato San grabbed the telephone and sent for Sergeant Ogura of the Aliens Branch.

"Sergeant, aren't you the man in my command who specializes in religious questions?"

The sergeant bowed, delighted to be called on for help by the great chief. His duties led him every day at service-time to the Christian churches of the town, where he listened to the sermons and checked up on the Japanese nationals in the congregation. Though a devout Buddhist and a faithful Shintoist, he nevertheless had contracted a passion for Christian church music during his rounds, particularly for the harmonium, whose strains, quite unlike anything in Japanese ceremonies, moved him to ecstatic bliss. He had also been so much impressed by the fervent eloquence with which Protestant clergymen read the Bible that, having acquired a copy of that precious book, he read long passages of it aloud at home in the evenings. Like all conscientious policemen who ultimately resemble their prey, Sergeant Ogura, without being converted, had acquired a clergyman's manner.

Sato San briefly outlined the situation. (Intelligent Japanese are quite capable of being laconic when they so desire.)

"If I may be allowed to offer a suggestion," said the sergeant in a smooth gentle voice, "I think the best thing would be to persuade the lady to build a small temporary chapel on the piece of land you are proposing to lend her. Kept between four walls and a roof, her zeal can offend nobody."

"A good idea, Sergeant Ogura, a very good idea! However, I can't help fearing that the possession of a chapel may encourage Miss Simpson to intensify her efforts at propaganda. You can't trust Christians. They build churches which you think are bound to stay empty. But on the contrary they always manage to fill them. It is hardly the function of the police to promote proselytism! Don't forget, either, that I shall have to recover the land after the lady goes."

"I understand perfectly, sir. And if need be, three or four people chosen by myself, with your permission, might form a congregation for the lady's sermons." (The sergeant assumed that the pious American was bound to preach sermons.) "I could even translate them."

"I won't ask you to go as far as that," said Sato San. "But since you speak English, you can be in charge of this affair. As of tomorrow, let there be no sign of a cross at the temple of Z——. And as this honorable lunatic must be kept quiet, offer her the piece of land, let her stay there with her chapel until we're rid of her and her nonsense. If you think a few figureheads would help to keep her there, get two or three maids from the inn. I'll warn the manager. But please, no scenes! We must offend neither the temple authorities nor the United States Embassy. See Miss Simpson as soon as possible. Of course you're released from other duties for the time being."

The sergeant took his leave. As he was going out, Sato San added a last word: "If Miss Simpson decides to build, see to it that her chapel doesn't look like a chapel, so that it can be converted later on into a police station."

"It shall be done, sir . . . A wooden house of seven or eight *tatami*, without windows or *shoji* . . ." He hesitated, and then added, "If the lady should wish to put in a harmonium, would there be any objection, sir?"

"No," said Sato San absentmindedly.

A harmonium? Why on earth? Sato San shrugged his shoulders and became absorbed in the study of General de Lure's dossier. Sergeant Ogura left police headquarters in a mood of serene satisfaction. He already fancied he could hear the strains of that harmonium.

The case of General de Lure presented a different problem. Sato San was under no obligation to the French Embassy. In any case there was nothing reprehensible about the general's interest in the mendicant soldiers. Sato San had repeatedly protested that such beggars in uniform constituted a blot on the memory of the late Imperial Army and should not be tolerated. His protests were in vain, and the thought infuriated him. How could the Chief Commissioner endure the sight of men, Japanese men, displaying their degradation in the streets of Tokyo? It was painful enough for any Japanese worthy of the name to see his country's new army parading in the khaki uniform of its conquerors, but that the other uniform, the real one, should be worn only by beggars was an intolerable insult. And now a stroke of luck gave him an opportunity to punish one of those wretches! His plan was Machiavellian, but it might succeed if he took charge of it in person. He barked an order into a telephone. A policeman burst in, saluted and stood to attention before his desk.

"Here's the address of a certain Hakayama San, a professional beggar. Arrange to get in touch with him. If he's not at home, inform the local stations. I want him to be found tonight, or tomorrow at the latest. Tell him from me that the honorable French general whom he met at the Yasukuni Temple the other day is anxious to visit him. As the honorable general is a person of considerable importance, Hakayama San must give him the best possible reception. I shall act as interpreter myself. He is to expect us at his home next Thursday afternoon. Impress on him that he is not to try to get out of this meeting. If I don't find him there, tell him he'll regret it, that I shall order him to be forbidden access to all temples. Inform me when this assignment is completed. You may go."

Then he telephoned the Pine Wind Inn. Mme. Hashi answered.

"*Anone!*" said Sato San. "I should like you to show particular consideration to Sergeant Ogura of the Aliens Branch. I have instructed him to keep an eye on the American lady who plants crosses, and who has already incurred the displeasure of the honorable Prior Toyota San. I strongly urge you, in the interests of your relations with the temple authorities, to help Sergeant Ogura fulfill his mission. I am greatly obliged to you." (At the other end of the line Mme. Hashi was tittering nervously.) "Will you tell the French general that I should like to speak to him. . . . Good morning, General," he went on in English, "I have made personal inquiries about Lieutenant Hakayama. I have found out where he lives, and he knows of your proposed visit. His home is in a distant suburb, very hard to find. It would be a great honor to me to accompany you, and since you speak English I shall be very glad to serve as interpreter for you— No, no, it's nothing at all! I am very fond of France and of the French. Indeed it's I who am grateful to you for giving me this opportunity to help you. If it is to your satisfaction, we will go on Thursday afternoon. My car will pick you up at the inn . . ."

He hung up, leaving General de Lure bewitched by his courtesy. Sato San smiled. These foreigners were proving quite a godsend, provided one knew how to deal with them. A sixteen-year-old *maiko* fit for a cabinet minister, congratulations from the Chief Commissioner, a car, a chauffeur, two armchairs, the right verdict in the Marshall case, a new police station to present to his superiors, the good opinion of the Prior of the Temple, the lasting gratitude of a teahouse owner and the probable punishment of an unworthy fellow countryman . . . all this in less than ten days! He might well be pleased with himself.

A few minutes later there was a hum of excitement in the gloomy corridors of Police Headquarters. Office doors opened, and a hundred pairs of eyes peeped out to watch Miss Cloudless Sky glide past in her red kimono. She tripped neatly up the stairs, followed by Mr. Miyamoto, somewhat embarrassed at finding himself in such spectacular company. The grimy walls of the police building echoed the tap-tap of her black lacquer *geta*. Inspectors bowed low to her. They had priced her kimono and assumed her to be the mistress of some high official. On the third-floor landing, terror seized Mr. Miyamoto. What did the redoubtable Sato San want with him? Why had he sent for the geisha? For the past two days the poor man had been losing weight and sleep. He had even given up studying George Sand. His series of misfortunes weighed him down. They surely betokened some mysterious vengeance on the part of his family gods. For, directly or indirectly, these calamities were due to members of his own family—to an officer on his late father's staff, to his sister Keiko, to his second cousin the geisha. He was trembling as he entered Sato San's office.

The policeman invited them to sit down with great courtesy. Miss Cloudless Sky was not used to armchairs. After sitting down she took off her *geta*, then knelt on the armchair and held herself erect, as if on a mat, which surprised nobody. Sato San complimented her on the sumptuous dinner which she had helped to organize. As she had not followed the American's speech and was ignorant of his real intention—the secret had been well kept—the geisha expressed her thanks, then spoke in flattering terms of her friend Miss Morning Mist, of whose liaison with the policeman she was well aware. Little Miyamoto was smiling frantically. Sato San's remark had really been intended for him. It meant, "I know perfectly well that that unspeakable dinner party was only made possible through your cousin's cooperation, and that you yourself urged her to accept." Miyamoto had not failed to understand. These few words spoken to the geisha in the most pleasant of tones meant that he lay more than ever at the policeman's mercy.

Having talked about nothing for ten minutes, as is proper in good society, Sato San asked suddenly, "Does Geisha San know the exact translation of the honorable American's speech?"

"I did not consider myself entitled to repeat it to her, honorable sir," quickly replied Miyamoto; "you told me not to."

"Just as well," said the policeman drily, "I'd never have forgiven you."

The little interpreter was on the edge of panic. Sato San watched him attentively with a terrifying icy glint in his half-closed eyes. Another minute, thought the policeman, and I'll get whatever I want from him. The moment seemed ripe.

"Repeat to your cousin, word for word, the speech of Cadwallader San."

Slumped in his armchair, looking like a culprit caught red-handed, and not daring to glance at his cousin, Miyamoto lived through his ordeal once more. His voice failed, his words would not come, he had to force them out one by one. When he came to the famous phrase—*We know the state of slavery in which you are kept against your will*—he stopped.

"I can't," he implored, "I can't translate it."

The fatal words would make him lose face in front of a woman, for his cousin would despise him for exposing her to such an insult.

"We're waiting," said Sato San, impatient to know the geisha's reaction. "Go on!" He was keeping the best role for himself.

Miyamoto mumbled through to the end. He was barely audible. Then, hiding his head in his hands, he burst into convulsive sobs. Sato San gloated for a moment over this sight, which confirmed the success of his maneuver; then, still impassive, he slowly asked, "And what does the honorable geisha think about it?"

Miss Cloudless Sky seemed quite unperturbed by these revelations. Being of better family and education than most, she realized that the life and functions of a geisha might seem strange and shocking to a foreigner. The equivocal character of her profession had not escaped her, whereas her companions, knowing no other moral code, had no suspicion of it. Miss Cloudless Sky, aware of these differences, made her living through men because they provided her with the luxury that was so scarce in postwar Japan. The other geishas did so unthinkingly, because their position required it and their Mama Sans insisted on it. She was a courtesan from ambition, the others from meekness. When she was bought from her parents as a little girl she had left her village well aware of the fate that awaited her, whereas most future *maikos* discover it gradually. Her father, a high official in Manchuria and a cousin of General Miyamoto, had lost all his possessions in the war. He had been forced to abandon his fortune, house and lands in Manchuria, which was now in the hands of the Chinese. Ruined, head over heels in debt, he had retired to a small farm near Kyoto belonging to his family, where he had cultivated his rice fields like the neighboring peasants. He was wholly unsuited to agricultural work, and the farm failed. He sold his wife's kimonos, mortgaged the house and then the lands. Threatened with foreclosure, he was forced to sell his daughter, but he did his best for her. He chose a Mama San of good reputation, a first-class *geishaya* in which the mistresses of several Cabinet Ministers had been trained, explained at great length to the little girl how, in the future, her power over men would enable her to succeed in life and escape from poverty, and promised, on leaving, to buy her back as soon as his affairs were in order. He died two years later of exhaustion and grief. His body was found floating in the liquid mud of his rice fields.

"I think," the geisha said after a thoughtful pause, "that the honorable American was not entirely mistaken."

The policeman leapt out of his chair. If the geisha meant what she said, the role of Madama Butterfly was hardly likely to suit her. Miyamoto looked up in amazement on hearing his cousin. Squatting on her armchair, as much at ease as though she were at a tea party, Miss Cloudless Sky surveyed her interlocutors with a serene smile.

"Does my reply surprise you? Yet you surely know, honorable sir, that our lives are circumscribed by the strictest of rules, from which very few of us succeed in escaping. It is ten years since my honorable father handed me over to Mama San, and my debt to her is still in the region of eight hundred thousand yen. Shall I ever find a *dana* rich enough to help me pay her back? And what's more, willing to do so? I'm not so sure, for times have changed. There's no lack of rich men in Japan, I grant you.

They organize big geisha parties because it is still the tradition among businessmen, and they give private suppers to their friends to which they invite us for a variety of reasons. But when they take a mistress their choice seldom falls on a geisha. They want a young woman with modern tastes, who can drive a sports car, wear Paris gowns as well as kimonos and bathe on fashionable beaches. Are geishas like myself capable of playing such a part? I doubt it. A geisha's place today is in the *ochaya* and nowhere else. Our life is a pleasant one. I don't regret it, I am even happy. When I look at myself in the mirror I tell myself that after all I represent the real spirit of Japan. Then I go out into the street and I see my country looking so different from myself that after a few steps around my house I quickly go back to the only setting that really suits me. And that is a sort of bondage. Do you not agree? That is why I said that the honorable American was not entirely wrong."

"Am I to understand," asked Sato San, somewhat disconcerted, "that you approve of his speech and his proposals?"

"Certainly not," she quickly replied, "although I wasn't in the least shocked by them. He simply failed to understand anything about geishas. There's no point in broadcasting such nonsense. It would only harm the traditions which we still represent."

For the first time since the beginning of their talk, Sato San felt able to relax. "If you were asked to accept his offer, what would you decide?"

"When such a rich man is fool enough to offer to build her a golden bridge, a wise woman will think twice before refusing."

They both laughed. Mr. Miyamoto drew himself up again, deciding that after all he hadn't lost so much face.

"Can I conclude from that," went on Sato San, "that you might eventually accept?"

"I answered your summons of my own accord, but before replying to the last question I should like to know why you sent for me. Did you intend to ask me to accept?"

The policeman thought it best not to conceal his motives. This geisha seemed too intelligent to be duped.

"It is a fact that the honorable Chief Commissioner attaches great importance to your collaboration."

He explained the affair in detail, stressing the condition laid down by the U. S. Embassy in the settlement of the Marshall case.

"You need a geisha, obviously. But why me? There were twenty-five of us at that dinner."

"It struck me that the honorable foreigner greatly enjoyed your company. He never took his eyes off you throughout the meal. You are the one person who can succeed easily, and who can prevent him from renewing his efforts. Our agreement with the Embassy specifically mentions one single geisha."

Miss Cloudless Sky rose and bowed, smiling. *In the future you will win success through your power over men,* her father had told her as he took his last leave of her. The time, it seemed, had come.

"One single geisha . . . Yes, indeed! Since the honorable American wishes to see me lead a free life, I won't disappoint him, but he'll have to pay a high price for it. To live a free life one has to be rich."

She was speaking in a soft indifferent tone as if discussing the weather. "Has he really as much money as you think?"

"Thousands of dollars! We checked his account at the Bank of Tokyo."

"In that case, by tomorrow maybe, if Mama San consents, I shall no longer be a geisha. Unfortunately I know very little English and Cadwallader San speaks no Japanese—"

"That doesn't matter," the policeman interrupted. Then he turned to Miyamoto: "You told me the other day that you wanted to become a journalist. The chief editor of the *Asahi* is a friend of mine. I shall recommend you to him. In the meantime, be kind enough to help your cousin, with all the discretion you have shown hitherto. The Geisha San's success is necessary to Japan's foreign policy. Consider it your duty to promote it."

"I shall always be most happy to serve my country," the little interpreter replied gravely. He had scarcely expected to be let off so easily.

Miss Cloudless Sky opened the office door. She had stopped smiling, and her features had hardened.

"I owe my country nothing," she said. "It let my father die after his long and faithful service. If I accept it's solely in my own interest. So the honorable Chief Commissioner may depend on my loyalty."

Sato San escorted them onto the landing, then returned to his office in a pensive mood. This easy victory depressed him. Gone were the days of heroic self-sacrifice. A bank account had done the trick.

Cadwallader, that very evening, triumphantly signed a check for a million yen made out to Mama San, who wept crocodile tears.

"I have answered your appeal," said the geisha, her black eyes fixed on the American's. He looks like a good trusty dog, she thought with a certain tenderness. "But I have given up my profession and my livelihood. What is to become of me?"

She was a touching, fragile figure in her red kimono. Miyamoto interpreted, and the American was deeply moved. The girl's sincere and trusting surrender set off a wild commotion in his heart, and it was with a faltering voice that he replied, "You have chosen liberty. America will never . . . I will never desert you. Sleep in peace. Tomorrow we will set about organizing your new life." He fled, unable to say another word.

Miss Cloudless Sky went off by herself to Akasaka and visited the geishas' hairdresser to sacrifice the heavy coils of her black hair. The skillful coiffeur made them into a wig which he sold for a good price. But as he cut off those glorious locks he could hardly repress his grief. He was quite sincere, in the Japanese fashion. . . .

In the inn parlor, Miss Simpson was holding council with the head carpenter and the head roof-tiler, both clad in short working tunics, one black and the other sky-blue, with great white letters on their backs. Sergeant Ogura, in plain clothes, led the discussion. A huge plan drawn in Chinese ink was spread out on the table. In graceful lettering the master carpenter had painted an inscription beneath it: TEMPLE OF UNKOWN AMERICAN RELIGION. The term New Baptist meant nothing to him, and he asked himself no unnecessary questions. He had been told to plan a rectangular house of ten *tatami*, with a Japanese roof and a single door but no *shoji*. In one day he had produced his plan. The foreign lady was in a hurry. All right, everything was ready. Japanese houses, being made of wood without foundations, are very quickly built. Miss Simpson was surprised to learn that the roof was built first, on six wooden uprights driven into the ground.

"And there," said the sergeant, pointing to a mark on the plan, "we shall put the altar where the big book stands. In this right-hand corner a small dais for talking to the congregation."

Miss Simpson assented, astonished to observe yet again how very learned the sergeant was in religious matters. She had only known him for two days and already she found him indispensable. When he first came to the inn she had been living almost like a recluse in her own room, distressed at the indifference that surrounded her and lacking heart for anything except prayer. Bad news from the minister at Burke City had further depressed her. The missionary who had been sent at great expense into Kashmir had failed to find the man she had converted, while the two dancing girls whom she had hoped to win for the New Baptist faith had tried to seduce him the first time they had prayed together. Grieved but resigned, the missionary had gone home to the United States. Feeling herself forsaken by God, Miss Simpson had barely listened to Sergeant Ogura saying: "The cross will have to be removed from the garden—the prior of the Temple has complained."

As she protested feebly he said in a tone of fervent conviction unconsciously copied from one of the ministers on whom he spied, "God moves in a mysterious way."

Heaven be praised! She had not prayed in vain. Here, providentially, was the willing apostle, the one just man who makes amends to a lonely missionary for any amount of suffering and ingratitude. What had he said next? That she was to build a chapel? Lord, I thank Thee for reminding me of my duty through the lips of this unbeliever whom Thy will inspires! Since it is Thy command, I shall build Thy church. She had promptly gone into the garden. Sergeant Ogura had dug up the cross himself with such respectful and almost tender care that Miss Simpson, in a transport of fervent gratitude, had taken to calling him Brother Ogura. Together they had visited the piece of land offered by some mysterious benefactor, at a crossroads near a market place. They had collected workmen, chosen timber and tiles, ordered seats, bought bilingual Bibles and hymnbooks.

"And finally," the sergeant had said, "here on the left we will put the harmonium."

They had ordered and paid for the instrument the day before at the American store in Tokyo. It was not as new as it might have been, having served in a field chapel during the Korean campaign, but the store had no other. Miss Simpson had thought it unworthy of her chapel and had proposed to order a new one from the States. But Brother Ogura had been so insistent. "Our congregation must learn to sing at the very first meeting." Our congregation! How well he understood what really mattered! Her eyes swimming with tears of joy, she had paid at once.

The head carpenter asked what sort of mat should be used. Sergeant Ogura reflected for a moment. In a police station you need a wooden floor—in a Christian church too, since worshipers don't take off their shoes.

"No mat," he said, "but a good strong wooden floor that will stand up to boots."

The head carpenter obediently made a note of this, meanwhile wondering vainly what made Christians put on boots to pray.

When the final details were settled, the four of them went to watch the work in progress. Two small three-wheeled trucks were already there. Workmen in tunics, with handkerchiefs knotted around their heads, were stacking up on the pavement, in regular pyramids, gray tiles and boards so smooth and neat that they looked like the shelves of some gigantic bookcase. Threads stretched from four poles, at a height of two yards, marked out the site. Each pole was adorned with a green branch of the holy *sakaki* tree. Paper streamers of yellow, red, blue, green and violet, the five sacred colors, hanging from the threads, fluttered gently between paper figures of suns and moons, horses and *tori,* like children's cut-outs. Three small saucers containing rice, salt and sake stood on the ground in the middle of the site, with a minute sprinkler of bamboo.

"Brother Ogura!" Miss Simpson called out, "this is all very pretty, it looks like a street fair, but what's the meaning of it?"

The sergeant tilted his head, scratched the back of his neck and uttered a long hissing sound, the Japanese symptom of perplexity. He realized in confusion that these preparations for driving out evil spirits did not exactly conform to the New Baptist creed. However, he told her. When she heard the explanation, Miss Simpson nearly jumped out of her skin. However, she promptly collected herself. With a missionary's long-suffering, she remembered that the heathen are just overgrown children, that you have to explain things to them carefully, in detail, so as not to leave in their minds those zones of darkness that weaken the foundations of conversion.

"What are you thinking of, Brother Ogura?" she said in a grieved but affectionate tone, as though chiding a child. "You know there are no such things as spirits. There is only one God. He lives in Heaven and judges all our deeds. What would He think of us, my brother, what would He think of you—for He sees us, He knows everything—if we consented to believe in evil spirits? Those ungodly devices must come down!"

Ogura did not want to rush things. The Christian God would undoubtedly protect his own church, but certainly not the police station. Nevertheless he consulted the head carpenter and his colleague, the head roof-tiler. Both stated categorically that none of the men would consent to work on the site unless the evil spirits were driven from it. No building, from the largest factory to the humblest wooden shed, goes up in Japan without these religious precautions. The spirits are immortal, and take no notice of progress. Even if one has ceased to believe in them they still exist. And when Japan builds its first atomic power station, you may be sure that a ceremony of purification will precede the laying of the foundation stone.

"All right," said Miss Simpson, "if they refuse to get rid of those papers I can do without them. Brother Ogura, we shall build the Lord's house with our own hands!"

Brother Ogura displayed a certain skepticism. He knew nothing about carpentry. Neither, for all her apostle's soul, did Miss Simpson. He told her so.

"You're quite right," she said. "I will sign on some American workmen. The Lord's law must reign over this heaven-sent plot of Japanese land, and your imaginary spirits will be driven out by Almighty God's power alone."

She bit her lip. This was not quite what she had meant to say.

The sergeant had an inspiration: "You've admitted yourself that the place must be delivered from evil spirits. I don't believe in these popular superstitions—(*Forgive me, O kami of earth and air!*)—but these workmen do. If your church is built by foreign hands, what Japanese will dare enter it? Leave these poor souls alone, and while they carry on their backward practices, you and I, Miss Simpson, will pray that your God alone may drive out the spirits."

Somewhat nonplused, Miss Simpson considered this peculiar form of competition. She was still worrying over it when a new figure startled her from her indecision. This was an old man bent with age, decrepit, his wizened face creased with wrinkles. A long-sleeved purple gown and a small black cap like a beadle's, surmounted by a strip of cloth of the same color rolled up into a ball, showed that he was a priest. He was carrying a sword. Two assistants in long white tunics and caps of black cloth walked solemnly behind him. These were the Shinto clergy of the district, come to purify the site. The head carpenter and the head roof-tiler greeted them with a display of profound respect, while the workmen, lined up behind, bowed to the ground.

"Who are these people?" Miss Simpson asked. "What are they going to do?"

She had a proper New Baptist's hatred of vestments. Sergeant Ogura grasped her by the arm.

"It's too late, Miss Simpson. The purification ceremony has begun. There's nothing we can do now without creating a scene."

Angelica closed her eyes, clasped her hands and stood motionless. Only her lips moved in prayer. The priest drew from his sleeve a fading parchment which he unrolled. It was a catalogue of all the beneficent *kami* of the neighborhood with their complete genealogies. He read it aloud in a monotonous quavering voice. From time to time he interrupted his enumeration to sing the praises of some particular *kami*, urging his listeners to worship them. A few women on their way back from the nearby market joined the crowd of workmen. They all watched the ceremony with seeming indifference, the workmen chatting to one another, leaving the specialists to cope with ritual, which was their job. At regular intervals the priest in the black cap seized the bamboo sprinkler, dipped it into the saucers and scattered sake, salt and rice over the ground. Miss Simpson went on praying.

Surrounded by so many gods at once, the spirits lost their hold and fled to other regions offering more scope to their malignity. One of them seemed to put up some resistance, however, for the old priest unsheathed his sword, a sharp, curved blade. He held it up at eye level and pivoted around several times, his purple robe sweeping the dust. Some children pushed their way into the front row. The old man motioned them aside with the tip of his sword. All at once he grew excited, brandished his weapon and mimed a fight. He leapt about like a young warrior, raising eddies of gray dust, and turned suddenly around with an angry gleam in his eyes, as if the enemy were attacking him from the rear. Miss Simpson, startled by the thud of his feet, opened her eyes. She closed them again immediately in horror and reverted to her silent prayer with even greater fervor. Brother Ogura observed that, for his age, the old man was still an efficient priest. The spirits were growing weary and the battle drew to a close. The swordsman flailed the air one last time and then sheathed his weapon, out of breath. He had conquered the devil. As a final precaution he grabbed a branch of *sakaki* and whipped the air around him. The last unholy emanations were scattered to the four winds. He withdrew, panting but dignified, followed by his two acolytes, one carrying the sword and the other the sprinkler.

Miss Simpson watched them go with a composure that surprised her. She had discovered tolerance.

Four days later, on Sunday April 22nd, the Japanese chapel of the New Baptist Church of Burke City, South Dakota, was completed. Sato San paid it a secret visit and thought it almost too elegant for a police station. It looked more like a teahouse, with its roof of finely worked gray tiles, its walls of polished wood and the terraces that surrounded it on three sides. The head carpenter, unacquainted with Christian church architecture, had in fact drawn his inspiration from the tea-drinking ritual. Miss Simpson was delighted. It was so picturesque, so Japanese, that it could not fail to attract the unconverted. She had made a tremendous effort toward sympathy and understanding, and now, with no more doubts as to the success of her mission, was confidently awaiting the opening service, which was to take place at six o'clock that evening.

During the morning a dozen benches were delivered, together with the dais and an altar consisting of three red lacquer tables piled one on top of the another. Miss Simpson laid on the altar a monumental Bible borrowed from the cultural department of the United States Embassy. The sergeant presided in person over the unloading and installation of the old harmonium. Two clumsy porters who dropped the precious instrument lost face under a shower of abuse from Brother Ogura. Miss Simpson had to calm him by playing a hymn. A few inquisitive onlookers, attracted by the unusual sound, gathered in front of the open door.

"The performance is at six," the sergeant announced, "free admission. There's going to be music."

They promised to come back. However, Ogura thought it wise to make sure of reliable supporters and went off to the inn to recruit some of the maids. Mme. Hashi considered it her duty as hostess to accept the invitation herself. In the meantime, Miss Simpson retired to her room to collect her thoughts and choose the psalms and hymns for this opening service, which she was to celebrate herself. According to the rules of the New Baptist Church of South Dakota any member, male or female, might perform a minister's duties in an emergency. She also wrote a long letter to David Wolf telling him the glad tidings— "We have lost Kashmir, but God in His goodness has given us Japan."

At six o'clock Miss Simpson, in a dark suit and a green hat stuck with daisies, entered her chapel. All the seats were full. Most Japanese are idle on Sundays, and the news of the meeting had flashed around the neighborhood. Mme. Hashi sat in the front row in her dressiest kimono, keeping an eye on her squad of maids. Miss Simpson took her place on the dais. Mme. Hashi wondered whether to clap, but as the sergeant made no movement she decided that the time had not yet come.

With shining eyes Miss Simpson opened her Bible and read in a warm, resonant voice: "Thus saith the prophet Isaiah: Arise, shine, for thy light is come, and the glory of the Lord is risen upon thee . . ."

Sergeant Ogura stood at the foot of the dais, looking very dignified, and read out, verse by verse, the Japanese translation given in his bilingual Bible. As the Japanese are highly sensitive to poetry, the lines: "The Gentiles shall come to thy light, and kings to the brightness of thy rising" called forth appreciative murmurs, and the reading went on amid general approbation.

Then came a puzzling passage: "The multitude of camels shall cover thee, the dromedaries of Midian and Ephah . . ." The thought of these shaggy creatures, which they had only seen at the circus, set the maids giggling delightedly behind their hands. A wave of laughter flowed through the congregation. The sergeant stumbled in his reading, slightly bewildered. In all the services he had attended, he had never heard people laughing before. But Miss Simpson's fervor was unperturbed. She soared to the heights of seraphic bliss. The last words of the lesson promptly re-established calm: "All they from Sheba shall come; they shall bring gold and incense; and they shall show forth the praises of the Lord."

Miss Simpson stepped down from the dais and took her seat at the harmonium, in front of the maids. Mme. Hashi admired her hat, but decided upon closer scrutiny that the daisies were artificial. The first chords aroused a flutter of curiosity. Everybody stood on tiptoe to see better. Children wriggled through to the front row and stood gaping with their fingers in their noses. Sergeant Ogura listened, his mouth open in a beatific smile. Then Miss Simpson sang the first hymn, carefully chosen for the occasion. She had a pleasant mezzo voice and was adept at playing the lush chords of the accompaniment.

> "God is working His purpose out as year succeeds to year,
>   God is working His purpose out and the time is drawing
>   near;
>   Nearer and nearer draws the time, the time that shall surely
>   be,
>   When the earth shall be filled with the glory of God as the
>   waters cover the sea."

Thus the service went on for an hour, lessons and hymns alternating. The atmosphere was pleasantly relaxed. People exchanged impressions with their neighbors, some preferring the harmonium and others the poetry, while all admired the foreign lady's voice. Miss Simpson listened indulgently to their chatter. "We must be happy in the Lord's house," she told the sergeant. At the end of the final hymn she stepped onto her dais again and made a little speech to the congregation, warmly inviting them to come back the next day, this time for instruction. On a signal from Ogura, Mme. Hashi put down the names of three of her maids. A girl who wanted to learn English, an old man who had nothing better to do, and the local police spy completed the list of postulants. She had netted six converts at her first try! Miss Simpson left the chapel in an ecstasy of grateful joy.

The sergeant stayed behind. "I'm going to put the seats away," he had explained. He closed the door, sat down at the harmonium and let his fingers stray at random over the keys. A storm of discordant sounds arose from the venerable instrument. Openmouthed, his eyes shut, Brother Ogura played on late into the night.

The New Baptist creed had made two people happy.

Sato San's *toyopet*, which had left the center of Tokyo an hour before, rattled over the beaten earth of the inextricable tangle of suburban roads. The driver, a blue-uniformed police corporal, had blind faith in his country's machinery. He made no effort to avoid pot-holes, bumps or open gutters, and just sat, firmly grasping the steering wheel in both hands. As there was no pavement, thousands of pedestrians thronged the roadway, busier than a swarm of ants—errand boys on bicycles, water carriers, housewives, peddlers, manure collectors—and hundreds of children. And on top of all the noise sounded the impatient honk of the *toyopet*, as the driver, foot on the accelerator, sped recklessly and with supreme indifference through the crowd.

"If this goes on we shall kill somebody," said General de Lure.

"No danger of that," Sato replied. "This is our best driver. He has been transferred from ambulance work."

The car emerged at last from the throng and turned right, down a dusty street that was less congested, then right, then left, then right again . . .

"Where are we?" asked the general.

"In northeast Tokyo." Then came a complicated name ending in "mura" which the general forgot as soon as he had heard it.

Actually the district where ex-Lieutenant Hakayama lived was due north. The car was traveling by a roundabout route by order of Sato San, so as to conceal landmarks and to make sure the general could never return by himself.

They turned left, then right, then left, then right again . . . No names on the streets, no bilingual signposts, thousands of small wooden houses all exactly alike and all equally squalid, so that the general had long since given up trying to find his bearings. At the district station they took on a waiting policeman.

"It is not far now," said Sato San, "he will guide us. It is very hard to find anyone in Tokyo. Only our policemen are able to do so."

The general was somewhat ill at ease. With all these policemen around him, his good deed was beginning to look like a man hunt.

"Do you think we will find him at home?" he asked.

"I am sure of it."

At last the *toyopet* stopped in an almost deserted street of dilapidated houses with newspaper over the windows. Three men of indefinable age, emaciated, barefoot, in tattered trousers gaping at the knees and stained and ragged shirts, stared vacantly at the car. They turned swiftly on their heels, apparently reluctant to engage in conversation.

"We're there," said Sato San.

Before them, between two cobblers' workshops, was a dark evil-smelling alley, thick with a layer of accumulated filth. Strips of bloodstained leather, partially tanned, were drying from a string stretched across the alley. One had to bend down to pass. If the general had been better acquainted with Japan he would have understood that he was in a *tokusu-buraku*, a pariah settlement, where the inhabitants, outcasts from Japanese society, carried on occupations once condemned by Buddhist religion and now despised by the rest of the population. One behind the other, following the local policeman who appeared to know the way, Sato San and the general ventured down the alley, which was so narrow that by stretching out one's arms one could touch the walls on either side. They emerged after a few steps into a minute muddy courtyard. Another policeman, in uniform, was waiting for them there, thus heightening General de Lure's uneasiness. The three officers consulted each other.

"As I promised you, Hakayama San is at home."

The general felt an urge to escape, to leave his overconspicuous and officious escort saying that he was tired, that he'd come back later . . . He wanted to help this man, not track him down like a criminal. He hesitated. Perhaps it was just an excess of good will?

"If you will please follow me," said Sato San, "we will go inside."

They passed through a rickety wooden door into a low room where the *shoji*, doubtless beyond repair, had been replaced by boards torn from packing cases. Tattered mats, a shabby mattress in one corner. Two women were squatting with a great pile of rushes in front of them, weaving baskets. They wore a sort of long white smock buttoned in front. Certainly not Japanese women, thought the general.

"They're Koreans." Sato San uttered the words with barely veiled contempt. Without even looking at the two women, Sato San snapped out a harsh order. They fled, leaving their baskets.

"Hakayama San!" he called out.

"*Hai!*" a voice replied from the next room.

No door opened. What a strange welcome, thought the general. The ex-lieutenant seemed reluctant to meet him.

Then he noticed that neither he nor Sato had taken off their shoes on entering the room. He untied his laces.

"There's no need. You'll only get your feet dirty."

Still the same tone of contempt! As for Hakayama San, he had given no sign of life since his earlier reply.

"Let's leave," said the general, disgusted with the outcome of his good intentions.

Sato San made no reply. The policeman who had been in the yard came in to join them. On an order from his chief he opened a door which revealed another room as poor and bare as the first. Hakayama San was kneeling in the middle of the floor, his single leg doubled up beneath him. The stump of the other was propped up on an old cushion. He made no movement, he did not even raise his head. An artificial leg of metal and a pair of crutches stood against the wall behind him. In one corner lay a pile of empty sake bottles. He had been told to be there, and he was there, alone. The five other beggars, his companions in misfortune, had thought it wiser to desert a house which attracted the police.

Sato San spoke to him. "General de Lure of the French Army has expressed a wish to help you. I hope you appreciate the immense honor he is doing you."

Hakayama San started. A general! They hadn't told him it was a general. Propelling himself on both hands (one of flesh, the other of leather) he crawled as far as the wall and slithered into an upright position. When he was standing propped up against the wall, gasping for breath, he found his crutches were out of reach. The general darted forward to hand them to him. Sato San had not stirred, neither had the uniformed policeman. Now, leaning on his crutches, the beggar stood erect in his white tunic and faced them. His one eye rolled wildly, unseeing. His breath reeked of sake. He had been drinking all morning in anticipation of this visit, but he was still sufficiently lucid to realize that the presence of this foreign general in the hovel that he, a lieutenant of the Imperial Army, shared with five mendicant soldiers and two Korean women placed the seal on his degradation.

"A drunkard!" said Sato San. "I am sincerely ashamed, sir, to have inflicted this repulsive spectacle on you."

The general clenched his fists, struggling against an overpowering desire to lash out at the smug, grinning face of the police official. He put all the authority he could muster into his request: "Please tell this officer . . . how deeply distressed I am . . ." He had a lump in his throat. "It's shameful," he added, "shameful!"

Sato San translated in his own fashion, in a low voice, as if unwilling for the general to understand the hatred and contempt his words implied: "The honorable French general wants me to convey his pity and the shame he feels for you."

Hakayama San stared at him. The effects of his liquor were beginning to wear off.

"Leave me alone," he said painfully, "leave me alone!"

"Not until I have said this to you," the policeman went on. "I am ashamed too, I'm ashamed when I think of all those who have died and of whose death you make a mockery! For your wounds aren't even war wounds. There was no fighting in the Kuril Islands! You bungled your suicide, you had the impudence to outlive your general, who was well aware that a man of honor cannot survive a war lost without fighting! If you even had the decency to hide yourself, if one didn't have to see you! But every day you insult the dead heroes in the temple of Yasukuni, and your mere presence teaches all the young people who visit the sanctuary, and on whom the hope of our country depends, that a Japanese soldier can go on living in shame. The police put up with you, but the Japanese people loathe you. You're accepted by none but outcasts, and by the lowest of them all, the Koreans!"

"Where am I to go?" asked the lieutenant. "No Japanese was willing to rent me a room." He drooped over his crutches, shaking with misery.

"When every man's curse is on you, there's nothing left but to die."

Sato San uttered the last sentence without hatred or scorn, as an appeal to reason and self-respect. His voice had grown almost gentle and compassionate, as though he were saying: "I'm grieved about it, but there is no alternative." An obscure feeling of pity stirred in the hidden depths of his soul. This beggar had suddenly come to represent all the forgotten misery of the defeated nation. He was almost on the point of speaking charitably, like that sentimental general. . . .

"We must go," he said in English. "I should not have brought you here."

There was a note of anguish in his voice. The beggar, propped on his crutches, in his white shroud, seemed a ghost. The shrill voice of one of the Korean women rang out in the yard.

"Are they soon going?" she asked a policeman. "I've got my baskets to finish!"

"You're right," said General de Lure, "it would be better to come back later."

He was conscious of an unexpected solidarity between the beggar and the two policemen. He felt like an intruder.

"Please give him this," he added, "I had it ready for him."

He handed the police official an envelope containing fifty thousand-yen notes. Without a word Sato San gave it to the beggar, who seized it in his leather hand and let it drop. The envelope opened and the notes scattered on the mat. Silence.

"A fine salary for an officer," said Sato San at last in Japanese. In spite of his secret pity he was playing his role to the end.

Hakayama San did not even glance at the money. Nothing mattered to him now. He only felt an overwhelming weariness. Outside, the Korean women were still shouting. General de Lure could stand no more. He left the room and fled into the alley.

As they drove home, he said to Sato San: "I'm afraid of what may happen to that man. Let us go back tomorrow morning."

Hakayama San, left alone, staggered over to a cupboard at the end of the room, trampling the scattered notes as he went. He opened it, took out an officer's sword with a gold-tasseled handle and went into the next room, where the two women had resumed their basketwork. They paid no attention to him, being used to seeing him withdraw into a corner, holding his sword and staring at it like some recovered treasure. For that matter, the beggars did what they liked in this house, on condition that they paid a handful of yen regularly. For two hundred yen, indeed, the younger woman was lavish with her favors. The old one gave hers gratis. She was in great demand. . . .

The old woman let fall her basket and screamed. Holding his sword with his one sound hand, Hakayama San had thrust it violently through the dividing wall, up to the hilt. He went back into his own room without a word. The blade protruded from the wall on the left, pointing upward, half a yard of gleaming steel.

The former lieutenant threw down his crutches, shouted *banzai* as if about to charge and let himself fall with all his weight against the sword. The blade pierced the lower part of his abdomen, but as his body slumped down it cut through his entrails and came out behind, a little on one side, under the short ribs. Blood spurted onto the mat. The two women fled howling. Hakayama San lay dying, stuck through like a huge fly in an entomologist's collection, with his arms dangling, his body bent, his solitary eye already glazed.

He died at nightfall, as policemen swarmed up the alley. An hour later, Sato San dashed up to the Pine Wind Inn.

"He has killed himself," he told the general.

"You're a monster! You drove him to it!"

For the first time in their acquaintance Sato San looked him straight in the eye. The general was astonished to see an unfamiliar serenity in his expression.

"For the honor of my country," were his only words.

The *toyopet* was waiting for them at the door. They took their seats in silence. The car drove off into the night, its siren screaming.

The outcasts' district was deserted. Three policemen were standing on guard beside their van in front of the alley. In the courtyard the two Korean women were discussing the event, dry-eyed. The lieutenant's body in its bloodstained tunic was stretched out on a bier. His single eye had been closed. The bank notes were still strewn over the mat. Sato San picked them up and said, "If you'll allow me, I shall use them to have a tablet inscribed to his memory in the temple of Yasukuni. He has deserved it now. I shall simply write that he killed himself in 1945, in the Kuril Islands."

Then he picked up the sword, which had been wiped clean, put it into its sheath and offered it to the general.

"This man had no relatives. You are the last person who ever showed him any kindness. This weapon is yours by right. One of the finest swords I've ever seen! Take it, or else the Korean women will sell it."

The general accepted the sword, gravely, with an almost theatrical gesture. It had been a momentous happening in his life, but later on he never talked about it. He followed the bier step by step as far as the van, so that the dead officer might be escorted on his last journey by one of his peers.

The van moved off, carrying the body of Lieutenant Hakayama of the Imperial Japanese Army to the municipal crematorium. Bareheaded, his sword in his hand, unconsciously standing at attention, General de Lure watched it disappear into the darkness. They were a couple of defeated soldiers, miserable defeated soldiers. One was alive and the other dead. A wave of depression swept over him.

When he got back into the car he was nothing but an old man. . . .

Suicides always occur in waves in Japan, and in the next few days about a dozen mendicant soldiers killed themselves. Others took their place at the temple of Yasukuni, crooks and swindlers, bogus soldiers wearing borrowed tunics, sham leather hands and removable plaster legs.

Hakayama San had died in vain.

In a large and comfortable fitting room on the seventh floor of the big Takashiyama department store, Miss Cloudless Sky, very much at ease, wearing a light gray check suit, seamless stockings and high heels, was turning around among the huge mirrors that reflected her figure from six different angles. She still walked with tiny hesitant steps as though impeded by her kimono. An uninformed spectator might simply have concluded that she was wearing new shoes, which in fact was the case. Brand-new, too, were her black lizard-skin handbag, her antelope gloves, her long-handled umbrella, her padded brassière (for she had a tiny bosom), a green nylon slip which had made her shout with laughter, and various indispensable accessories such as a compact, a cigarette case, a lipstick in a silver holder, a pocket comb. It had taken all of three long afternoons to buy these various unfamiliar objects, three eventful joyous afternoons during which she gradually acquired self-confidence. With her short hair lightly waved, her new and subtler make-up, her red nails and her enormous black eyes, she was unrecognizable, but still enchanting. Nothing was left of the former geisha but that inimitable grace of gesture which enhanced her charm.

The fitter was all attention. This one young woman, invariably accompanied by a silent Japanese and a tall talkative American in high spirits, had in the past three days bought a complete wardrobe from her, including a winter coat, although the cherry trees were already in bloom. Three assistants stood by with pins and pieces of chalk, uttering cries of admiration.

Douglas Cadwallader IV, sitting squarely in an armchair with a cigarette in his hand, was experiencing the joys of the Creator. This adorable Eve was his own work! Leonardo da Vinci, the enchanter Merlin, Christian Dior—he was all these, and more. He had created beauty. He had renewed a soul! Like an artist enamored of his painting, he gazed at her with delight. She smiled at him, but her smile had changed too. It was triumphant, dazzling, almost hard, the smile of a woman who was sure of herself.

"Fabulous, Michiko!" (Miss Cloudless Sky had dropped her geisha name and reverted to her own.) "You're fabulous! When I think that only four days ago— But of course we decided not to speak of that. The past is done with, dead, and buried! The future's waiting for us!"

Miyamoto, his face inscrutable, translated word for word, scrupulously, as Sato San had commanded.

160

"You're looking glum, old man!" Cadwallader slapped him on the back. "You ought to enjoy life, it's the secret of success! I'm going to change your outlook for you! We'll have dinner together this evening and have a fine old time!"

The little Japanese coughed and drew a deep breath before venturing a tremendous laugh. The fitter and the salesgirls imitated him politely and painstakingly. Miss ex-Cloudless Sky, indifferent to all the noise, stood at the mirror, trying out the effect of her pretty legs in various poses.

"That's fine!" exclaimed Cadwallader. "You see, life's great!"

Another backslap. Miyamoto tottered. What humiliations he must endure before getting that job on the *Asahi!* All day long he had to translate such nonsense, such crazy declarations, such insulting allusions to time-tested customs, at the risk of losing face ten times an hour in front of servants, salesgirls and chauffeurs, and in front of his cousin, who pretended not to notice. A fine bitch she was! This was the price he must pay for a journalist's job. Drawing fresh courage from that hope, he burst into still louder laughter.

"What d'you think of your cousin? Isn't she amazing? The prettiest woman in the world!"

Douglas winked. Miyamoto imitated him with a painful grimace. Then the American took the girl by the hand and led her through the room, taking endless delight in seeing her walk at his side, now that she was at last worthy to be seen and shown. Michiko had gained poise, she walked with a firm steady step, held her chin high and gazed into the distance.

"This suit is perfect, I'll take it," she said to the fitter. "May I, Douglas?" she added in English. They were the first words she had learned.

The fitter thanked them profusely. The three salesgirls bowed. Michiko instinctively responded with a very low geisha's bow.

"Come now," said the American, "none of your Japanese nonsense! That's all over and done with."

Miyamoto translated calmly, in a dry impersonal tone that

clearly conveyed that he was not responsible for such remarks. The ex-geisha rose, nodded briefly to the astonished saleswomen and went out swiftly, followed by her escort. Cadwallader retraced his steps to hand the fitter a tip. It took the good woman thirty seconds to discover that she had a thousand yen in her hand. She caught up with him by the elevator and gave him back his money. He shrugged his shoulders and concluded that the Japanese would never get rich.

At the ground-floor counters, Michiko bought a gold bracelet, a bottle of perfume, a suitcase, a silk scarf and some lingerie. Then she calmly pulled out of her bag a list she had drawn up after studying catalogues and fashion magazines, ticked off the articles she had just bought, checked up on the remainder and then said, "There, that's all! Douglas San, you're a dear. You've given me the greatest joy of my life."

Her cousin translated in low tones, for the shop was crowded. In the street some American tourists turned to look at Michiko. One of them gave a whistle of admiration. And Douglas realized how happy he was. What a marvelous adventure he was having! He had forgotten all about his crusade. And yet, the first two days, he had been worried at seeing no more repentant geishas turn up. Miss Cloudless Sky had seen to that.

"They're waiting," she explained, "to find out if you're really going to keep your promises before they decide. The poor girls have already been let down so often that they dare not believe in such luck. When they discover that I have really become a free and happy woman, then they'll take courage. But it will take time. It won't do to rush things. Above all, don't attempt to renew your offer. Every Mama San would rise up in protest! And you'd only do my friends harm by trying to save them too fast. . . ."

He forgot the geisha problem, and fell in love with her.

The three of them dined at Loemeyer's, a German restaurant in the Ginza district. Rollmops, Vienna sausage and fried potatoes with good Munich beer, a table spread with a white cloth, armchairs, spoons and forks and table napkins. He seemed bent on Westernizing her. She made a few mistakes at first. She dropped her knife. She mashed her potatoes. But the restaurant was full of foreigners, and she watched them carefully throughout the meal. The result was surprisingly effective. She left half her sausage, wiped her lips delicately with the corner of her napkin and sat with her elbows on the table and her hands clasped under her chin. Since that morning Douglas had been turning over a sentence in his head, but it wasn't easy to say intimate things when they had to be interpreted by Miyamoto. The little fellow seemed in a good mood. He had drunk a great deal of beer and was belching with satisfaction.

"Miyamoto, old man," said Douglas, "you're a good friend of mine. I've something important to tell you— In my country, you know, we always speak straight from the shoulder."

The little Japanese waited with narrowed eyes.

"I won't beat about the bush." He stared into his plate. "I love your cousin. That may seem odd to you—a former geisha! but don't get me wrong. I respect her enormously."

Mr. Miyamoto squirmed in his chair. He could understand this lunatic loving his cousin, but as for respecting her!

Douglas thought he discerned incredulity in Miyamoto's attitude. He protested sharply: "Yes indeed, believe me, I do respect her! Her past life doesn't exist as far as I'm concerned. I respect her so much that my deepest wish is to make her my lawful wife! Well, I suppose that surprises you?"

"I appreciate the honor," Miyamoto replied after vainly trying to understand this sensational development.

"I'm leaving for America quite soon, in a week. I've got to speak to her right now, and you're the only person who can help me."

Douglas called the waitress and had their glasses refilled.

"You're not bored?" he said to Michiko.

"Not at all," she answered, when the remark had been translated. "Your presence is enough to keep me happy."

She was divine, he told himself for the hundredth time. He leaned toward Miyamoto, breathless with impatience. "Go on, tell her now! I can't bear this uncertainty any longer. Tell her I want to take her back to America with me. If Michiko can be happy in my country and will have me for a husband, we'll get married. Otherwise I won't try to keep her, she can come back to Japan as soon as she likes . . . and I'll be the most miserable man on earth . . . Translate all that, but do it nicely, gently, don't scare her! Make her realize that she's absolutely free to decide for herself, that she owes me nothing, that I want her love and not her gratitude . . ."

He looked like a small boy trying to please somebody and watching anxiously for the smile that would reward him. Mr. Miyamoto listened to his exhortations patiently, more moved than he cared to admit to himself. This wasn't easy to translate! But after all it was none of his business. He turned to his cousin and began: "*Anone!* . . . Cadwallader San . . ." and so forth.

Miss Cloudless Sky listened quite unperturbed. For the past two days she had been expecting some sort of declaration. But the offer of marriage surprised her. She put her hand over the American's, as she had seen a foreign woman doing at a nearby table.

"Maybe," she said in Japanese.

She smiled at him, the sweetest of geisha smiles. Douglas felt his heart miss a beat. What had she said?

"Maybe," Miyamoto translated. He took the word to imply a refusal. In his heart he disapproved of his cousin's game, although he could understand her wanting to play for time.

"Hurrah!" cried Douglas. His joy was a pleasure to see. "Let's all three go and celebrate! You must come to the States too, Miyamoto, we'll invite you over, I promise we will—eh, Michiko?"

This time Miyamoto had not the heart to interpret. They visited two or three bars together, danced at the Crown (the night club with three hundred hostesses), and parted late at night in front of the Marunuchi Hotel, to which the American had now moved. "No more Japanese nonsense!" Such was Cadwallader's program. He had therefore installed the geisha in one of the Marunuchi's finest rooms, far removed from the baneful influences of her past life. His own bedroom was three doors away. They parted outside the elevator, under the ostensibly indifferent eye of the Japanese pageboy. Without their interpreter, they had nothing more to say to each other.

Mr. Miyamoto returned to the inn where Liliane Laage, Nicole Marchand and the Englishman, Brownley, were still halfheartedly sight-seeing and required his presence each morning. The three last days of this curious week were spent visiting the Great Buddha of Kamakura, the Imperial Palace, a wrestling match where the champions, two mountainous men, looked like huge hairless babies, and walking through the endless corridors of the Ueno Museum between rows of fans and six-armed statues. Nevertheless Miyamoto managed to escape for long intervals and rush to the aid of his cousin. Miss Cloudless Sky, transfigured, was tasting all the joys of modern life. She had learned to sleep in a bed. Hugging a soft pillow, she ordered her breakfast by telephone. She played indefatigably with the nickel-plated faucets in her bathroom and changed her dress three times a day. A rich Japanese who owned a big store in Osaka took an interest in her. They met every evening at the bar. He wore well-cut, expensive Western suits, spoke fluent English and drove a Cadillac. Cadwallader liked him and enjoyed chatting to him over a drink as they sat in the huge hotel armchairs, Michiko perched gracefully between them, her legs crossed high, her hand hanging limply over the arm of her chair.

The second evening the man from Osaka had asked her promptly, without useless formalities, in Japanese, "The honorable American says he's engaged to you. It doesn't seem likely to me. What's the real relationship between you?"

Miss Cloudless Sky thought for a moment.

"Nothing," she said simply.

Then they spoke of other things. Next evening, while Douglas was in his room, the man made himself clear.

"One of my models had to leave. Her job is vacant. So is her apartment. Would you like them?"

He seemed utterly self-confident. The geisha knew these rich businessmen well. She had served them for several years as a docile courtesan, with old-fashioned humility. Today she faced them as an equal, wearing the same Western uniform. In that modern setting the ancient customs seemed blurred and unreal.

"I don't deserve such an honor," she said with a smile, "but I shall try to prove myself worthy of it."

"Tomorrow morning at nine I shall be taking the train for Osaka. A seat will be reserved for you. If you don't change your mind I shall be glad to see you there. I'll wait for you near the dining car."

"I shall be very happy to accept," said the geisha with a slight bow.

The American appeared, with a cheerful grin on his face and a handful of cigars in his hand.

"The best I've come across! Straight from Havana!" he said. "Take some for your journey . . . Yes, please do! It's a pleasure to offer them to you! I've quite a store of them."

"Many thanks," said the Japanese. He put the cigars in his pocket.

Mr. Miyamoto joined them later. Michiko took him along to her room and informed him of her proposed departure for Osaka.

"Couldn't you wait until he's left Japan?" he said. "The man's a fool, but he's goodhearted. He really loves you. Think of all he's done for you!"

The past two days had imperceptibly revived Miyamoto's loyalty to the Western clan. Cadwallader's naïve sincerity touched him as much as his pride, his tactlessness and self-confidence had shocked him. This American was a weak creature who could not hide his feelings. He was in for a cruel disappointment.

"No, really," he added, "he doesn't deserve such ingratitude!"

"I shall leave tomorrow," the geisha said, "for now I am free,

free to seize my opportunity. And that means the nine o'clock train to Osaka. Give him this parcel tomorrow, after I've gone. Until then, not a word. Go home to bed now. But as you go past the bar tell Cadwallader San to come and speak to me . . . I'm not ungrateful," she said with a strange smile. "Good night, cousin. If I have any success in life, I won't forget you."

Three minutes later Douglas knocked at her door.

"You sent for me, Michiko, here I am. But of course, you don't understand me, and your cousin's gone home . . ."

He stood helplessly in the doorway. Miss Cloudless Sky bade him enter, locked the door, unhooked the telephone, turned down the lights, then standing on tiptoe crushed his lips in a kiss so prolonged and passionate that it left him breathless and light-headed.

"I'm not ungrateful!" she whispered in Japanese.

They tumbled onto the huge bed. She knew men, white or yellow. Seven years of experience bore fruit that night. She was heaven and hell in one. When morning came Cadwallader had experienced all the sins and all the joys of the world.

Worn out and blissful, he staggered back to his room and sank into unconscious sleep, like an animal.

At nine A.M. the Osaka train left the Central Station of Tokyo. At one of the dining-car tables Miss Cloudless Sky, formerly of Akasaka, ate breakfast opposite her new master. Was she a free woman? Undoubtedly. She had chosen him herself.

Two hours later Douglas Cadwallader IV untied the ribbons of the parcel which Mr. Miyamoto, looking deeply embarrassed, had presented to him. It contained a pale blue silk kimono embroidered with birds and flowers and three exquisite tortoiseshell combs, which she had worn on the evening of the historic dinner party.

"Has she gone?" asked Douglas.

The little Japanese hung his head.

"I knew she would," said Douglas. "I knew it last night."

There are some nights of love that have no future. Miyamoto hunted for consolatory phrases.

"Don't go to so much trouble," said Douglas. "The more one gives the less one gets. That's one of the laws of life."

He closed his eyes. Memories crowded in, so vivid that he blushed—and he realized that he had told a lie. For he had been given a great deal.

He left Japan that evening. In the plane, under the bright pencil of light from the small lamp above his seat, he began his report to the Managing Committee of the Anti-Slavery League of the Sons of the American Revolution:

Our moral principles are not valid for Japan. Any undertaking that disregards this essential fact is inevitably doomed to failure. . . .

America, however, believes in the universality of its moral principles. His report aroused a general outcry.

He was forced to hand in his resignation.

In the *karate* champion's house, three men waited excitedly—Asaki San, the host, Matsuko San the camera merchant and Nakagawa San the local doctor—quaffing great draughts of sake and relating their sexual prowess. The *shoji* and the shutters were closed. The maid had been sent home for two days. From outside, the house looked deserted. They were expecting Liliane Laage for a farewell tea party. A tea party! The three men shouted with laughter. In the next room a double *futon* had been laid out like a boxing ring. Expectation made their eyes glitter. Nakagawa San and Matsuko San knew the Frenchwoman only from their friend's descriptions, but the tales they had heard in the public baths had set their imaginations ablaze. Sake? . . . Sake! . . . and they drank, and they impatiently nibbled their grilled rice *sembe*.

An alarming thought struck the doctor. "Suppose she brings an action against us?"

"Brings an action? You're crazy! Did you bring an action when your daughter was assaulted by that American soldier? You took good care not to, and I can well understand. Family

168

honor isn't the business of law courts. In any case, does a woman lodge a complaint if she's been a willing party?"

"But suppose she refuses? We aren't going to knock her senseless, are we?"

"Of course not, you fool! I know her. She'll take it more or less willingly! After all, she consented to come and she knows what to expect."

"From you, yes, but what about us?"

"Do you want to avenge your daughter or don't you? Would you not like the whole neighborhood to have a good laugh at the foreigner when they hear about it, and despise her as your daughter was despised? You would? Well then, nothing is easier! The rest is up to you! Come now, it is not the first time we've had a tea party together! The fact that our lady guest isn't Japanese doesn't make much difference!"

All three burst into a raucous laughter. Each was planning his own vengeance: Asaki San for having been flouted by this woman after he had held her at his mercy; Nakagawa San for the shame of his daughter whom one of these foreigners had dishonored; and Matsuko San for the pain and jealousy he felt at the seduction of thousands of Japanese women by their white conquerors. This one could pay for the rest. . . . Vengeance? Or rather opportunity. As the three of them in their loose evening kimonos knelt around the table with cups of sake in their hands, their hearts throbbing with unbearable excitement, each was obsessed by the thought of the exotic foreigner, defenseless.

A bell tinkled in the garden. A step sounded on the path. Asaki was left alone, as the two accomplices hurried into the next room.

Liliane waited outside the door. No light showed through the closed shutters. It's very dark and deserted, she thought. Then she remembered Miyamoto's advice: *"Beware of Sensei Asaki."* She shivered delightedly in apprehension. At last, for the first time in a week, she wasn't bored! The unexpected invitation, from a man whom she'd humiliated, the sinister gloom of this house, the anxiety that made her flesh tingle. . . . Adventure? She shrugged her shoulders automatically. An adventure with Asaki? She knocked on the door.

The athlete stood before her. Under his newly shaven scalp his face was like a bulldog's muzzle. A regular executioner's head, she thought as she entered. They knelt down on the mat.

"*O cha,*" he offered green tea, "*o sake,* whisky?"

She could not see his eyes between their half-closed lids, but she could feel them riveted on her, on her sweater, her shoulders, her neck, her legs. In the profound silence that filled the room, there was something terrifying about the lust of this silent, massive and motionless man. She broke into a deep nervous laugh.

"Whisky," she said, "a big glass."

In the next room, holding their breath, the two Japanese waited for their signal. What was Asaki doing? Was he going to call them or wasn't he? The Frenchwoman's laugh ran through them like a red-hot needle.

The clatter of glasses sounded like a thunderclap. Liliane emptied hers at one draught. Asaki in his eagerness spilled part of the bottle on the table. One second longer, she thought, and he'll burst! She had known many men in her life, of all colors and of all nationalities, but never before had she so keenly enjoyed her sense of power. The Japanese clenched his fists and an intense light gleamed in his black eyes. He seemed ready to leap at her. Then she gave him a long slow stare that conveyed defiance, desire, entreaty. She stood up.

"Come on," she said hoarsely, "come on!"

She slowly took off her sweater and walked towards him. He took her by the wrists and forced her to her knees. She surrendered. She felt Asaki's enormous hands run over her body. They rolled over on the mat. It was over very quickly, but this time she cried aloud with pleasure. Unable to control themselves any longer, the other two burst in. They took off their kimonos and, carrying her into the other room, threw her on the *futon.* She cried out again, then her cry turned into a long moan.

When they were sated they picked up their kimonos, exultant at the wonderful tale they'd have to tell in the neighboring bathhouse, drinking great gulps of whisky and sake. Then she rose from the *futon* where she lay. Her hair hanging loose, her eyes wild under heavy lids, magnificent in her nakedness, she came forward, her shoulders still heaving with suppressed sobs. She went up to Nakagawa and, fastening her arms around his body, she pressed herself against him. They watched her, in bewilderment. She ought to hate them, to shrink from them, to run away and hide for shame. On the contrary she was inciting them on, drawing Nakagawa down onto the *futon* from which she had just risen.

Their vengeance was slipping from them. They had become mere playthings in their turn. Where were the shame and scorn they'd longed to inflict? And when Nakagawa, exhausted, fled crestfallen into the dark street, when Matsuko collapsed in a drunken stupor a little later on and she found herself alone with Asaki, she burst out laughing and held out her arms, saying, "You poor silly little fool, why did you wait so long?"

He could not understand her words, but he knew now that his plan had gone awry. He carried her into his room, and they slept in one another's arms.

Liliane lived with him until the end of her stay. Tamed, stripped of all his pride, his resentment melted away by insatiable desire, the *karate* champion, former terror of the Philippines, served the Frenchwoman like a faithful lackey.

Each evening at dusk two silent shadows crept furtively into the house.

Asaki put up with them, for without them, he suspected, he would never have had this woman. He realized this on the last evening when, at his request, they stayed away. She met him with cold indifference and looked around the house with a searching glance.

"So your friends aren't there? Well then, good-by, my little Mongol!"

171

He tried to draw her onto the ever-ready *futon*. She slapped his hands and ran off into the garden, as remote as in the days when they had first met.

"*Sayonara!* Good-by!" she called from the distance, bowing slightly in the Japanese fashion.

"*Sayonara!*" he replied. And all his hatred came back. But it was too late. Waving good-by, she smiled at him for the last time and disappeared. Alone with his resentment, he stood silent for a few moments. Then, like any Japanese who wants to save his face, he burst into a tremendous laugh.

VI

Okinoshima

End of April

At the Pine Wind Inn, Germain wandered about like a lost soul. Keiko San had been gone a fortnight; she had disappeared "somewhere in the west." Since then, not a word, not a sign of life. Mr. Miyamoto avoided his company. Their relationship was confined to essentials. Confronted with the little man's barrage of inscrutable smiles, Germain had given up asking questions, since he always got the same reply.

"My sister is very well, thank you, but her aunt is still ill. She has to stay there and she asks me to send you her respectful regards."

They now exchanged only anodyne remarks on practical matters, in which neither was in the least interested. Miyamoto took up his duties punctually each morning, bowed invariable assent to Germain's instructions and bustled off to some landmark in Tokyo with the surviving tourists.

Only Nicole Marchand and Cecil Brownley seemed still to take an interest in Japan, and even so the honorable gentleman found it hard to tear himself from the willing arms of charming Tomoko San, Miss Prudence.

A queer end to the holiday, thought Germain as he watched the diminished group set off for its daily outing. The inn, the setting, the personnel were still there; the unfamiliar atmosphere selected for the trip was unaltered; the actors were in their places, all dressed up and living their parts; and the clients who had chosen "A Month in the Land of the Rising Sun" seemed to have got what they wanted. The Agency had scored a complete success—too complete indeed, like a comedy written to raise laughter which, to the author's amazement, draws forth tears as well. Cadwallader, that good guileless soul, had suddenly fled from Japan to escape his disappointment. General de Lure had shut himself up in his room until the time should come for the party to leave, haunted by the thought of that mutilated corpse for which he felt himself responsible, that symbol of all defeated armies. Miss Simpson had been thoroughly hoodwinked. These three had found out the truth, or would find it out sooner or later. Japan has no use for Westerners who are too sincere. They interrupt its play-acting.

For Japanese life is an elaborate comedy. Inflexible customs, concern with saving face, hypertrophied pride, insincerity exalted into a virtue, an obsolete conception of honor, the desperate quest for perfection, an arrogant national self-consciousness, a frantic fear of being misunderstood combined with a longing for nobody to understand—all these factors, plus innumerable contradictions, make up this many-sided comedy of which the rules and the plot are so involved that foreigners can only watch from the outside, spectators. Westerners who seek to participate are like specks of dust that throw the machinery out of gear.

All this became clear to Germain. The legendary Japan that he had planned to offer his clients, the Japan of temples and paper houses, geishas and warriors, gardens and kimonos, that refined, seductive, deliciously polite Japan was the real thing. He had merely forgotten that the country was inhabited by real people and not by dream figures. And the dreams he had carefully constructed for his visitors had turned into unfortunate realities.

But Liliane Laage and Cecil Brownley, surely, had got all they wanted? Germain could not reproach himself on their accounts. Their satisfaction would be short-lived, no doubt, but at least it would involve no disillusionment. Obviously! He gave an involuntary smile. Those two had chosen sensual pleasure, the only resource with which Japan was naturally lavish.

One failure, however—Nicole Marchand, although she was a model tourist and no trouble at all. She had seen everything and taken an interest in everything, conscientiously and even intelligently, but she did not like Japan. Her first impression had persisted throughout her stay. It was one of penury, squalor, ugliness and gloom. The Japanese charm had not worked. After Keiko San's departure he had taken her around once or twice, trying to communicate something of his own enthusiasm.

"Yes, it's pretty," Nicole had said, "of course it's pretty! A bit of garden, the line of a rooftop, a lantern, a tree against the sky, a face . . . You can glean bits here and there, but for the most part how dingy and depressing it all is! This country reminds me of a wilting rose bush with few flowers and a lot of thorns. Of course, you're prejudiced. Japan, for you, means a woman, an enchanting woman I admit, but still . . . Forgive me for asking you this, you love Japan because Keiko San is Japanese, that's quite natural. But are you sure you don't, in fact, love her just *because* she's Japanese, because her charm, her physical appearance and her ways are ideally Japanese and correspond to your preconceived picture of Japan?"

She had said it very nicely, but he had not replied. He did not know what to reply. He was uncertain. What if he himself had been caught in his own trap, taken in despite himself by the exquisite setting he had so deliberately sought, into which Keiko San fitted so naturally with her pretty kimonos, her charming expression, her limpid voice and her fragile loveliness. When she was beside him his dream of Japan seemed real. But one cannot live a dream; one always ends by waking up. . . . Alone in the inn, he turned over his problem for the hundredth time. "If I've got to be convinced," he decided at last, "I'd like it to be in her company." Late that afternoon Miyamoto came back, smiling and remote.

"Let's stop this game," Germain told him. "I'm leaving in two days. You'll never see me or hear of me again." He grasped the Japanese by the shoulders and forced him to look at him. "Just for once, give me a straight answer. Where is your sister?"

Mr. Miyamoto understood that any further evasion would be a grave breach of politeness. He saved his face: "Her aunt is much better," he laughed. "Keiko San will be delighted to see you. She is with my cousin at Okinoshima, a little island on Lake Biwa. Everyone knows her there, you've only to ask . . ."

His features were distorted by continuous hysterical laughter. For the first time, Germain remembered having thought him ugly. He felt a strong desire to slap his face. Oh, that laugh, that laugh! It was beyond bearing. . . .

That same evening he took the night train to Otsu on the shore of Lake Biwa.

The pointed boat sped forward in the early morning light. It was cold. The sun had not yet risen above the ring of hills. The surface of the lake was calm and unwrinkled, the purr of the motor muffled by the mist. From time to time there was a hurried rustle of wings and a bird's cry as a wild goose flew away. Germain, sitting in the prow of the boat on a pile of nets, pulled up the collar of his coat. He dipped his hand into the water and withdrew it hastily. The water was icy. The fisherman, standing in the stern with his knee pressed against the tiller, gave a friendly smile and spoke a few words in Japanese. He must have been referring to the cold. Germain was shivering, weary after a sleepless night in the train and a long hunt on the shore of the lake, in the damp fog of dawn, for a fisherman willing to take him to Okinoshima. The man threw him an old leather coat lined with sheepskin. On their left there emerged from the mist a worm-eaten wooden *torii*, sticking up in the water like a gigantic birds' perch.

"Okinoshima, one hour," said the fisherman, holding up one

176

thumb to make it clear. He was an old man, lean and bowed, with a scraggy neck and a deeply wrinkled brown face. His pointed cap with earflaps, his thick padded tunic, his baggy trousers tied tight at the ankles and his bare feet seemed to belong to a bygone age.

"Kanehira," Germain said.

"Me?" said the fisherman, pointing to himself. He seemed flattered.

In a famous $n\bar{o}$ play the warrior Kanehira, who lost his life in the battle of Awazu on the shore edge of Lake Biwa, appears to pilgrims in the form of an old boatman. . . . They both laughed. Toward eight o'clock the mist lifted, disclosing at the far end of the lake the dark green mass of Mount Hei, from which, for many centuries, soldier-priests by the thousands threatened the old imperial city of Kyoto. A cold breeze blew, stirring wavelets that broke with a splash against the side of the boat. The fisherman grasped the tiller in his hand.

"Okinoshima," he said, pointing.

Germain turned to look. There was the island, two or three hundred yards away—a miniature temple with curved roof, a few twisted pines, wooden huts clustering along the shore—a perfect Hokusai print. The boat moved alongside a stone jetty and entered the tiny harbor, meeting other fishermen on their way out to sea, all wearing the same thick tunics and caps with earflaps. Germain stood up and looked for Keiko San among the women moving busily about the narrow wooden quay. He did not see her. Why should she be expecting him? She did not know he was coming and perhaps she did not want him to come. Germain paid the old man and showed him on his watch that he wanted to go back at five in the evening.

"*Hai, hai!*" said the fisherman. He seemed delighted. Germain, seeing him so good-tempered, inquired, tapping the old fellow on the chest, "Okinoshima?"—did he live on the island?

"*Hai,*" repeated the fisherman.

"Miyamoto Keiko, Miyamoto San, *koko deska* [where is she]?" asked Germain in his halting Japanese.

The man shook his head to show his ignorance and turned away. That was odd, thought Germain, the island isn't so very big. He jumped to the quay, between two groups of women who were loading nets onto the boats. In their blue tunics and baggy trousers, with handkerchiefs knotted around their heads, they looked most unlike their city sisters. Germain went up to them, wondering how to begin.

"*Konishiwa* [good morning]," he said with a bow.

He was conscious of his awkwardness, but it did not deter him. The women stared at him good-naturedly with friendly smiles on their broad flat faces. They returned his bow, without unnecessary exaggeration. He asked, "Miyamoto Keiko San, *koko deska?*"

A flutter of excitement ran through the group, as though someone had startled an aviary. There was a muttered consultation. One of them came up and spoke a few words in Japanese which he did not understand. Then he had an idea. Pointing toward the west of the island, he repeated his question. "*Ihe* [no]!" said the woman. He pointed northwest. "*Ihe!*" Then north. "*Ihe!*" Northeast, then east. "*Ihe, ihe!*" To the south lay the lake. The woman looked appalled. He shrugged his shoulders and walked off down the narrow lane at the end of the quay.

A few yards away he came upon a house that was larger than the rest. A bulletin board and a Japanese flag gave it an official air. Was it the town hall or the harbor office? He went in. A man of about forty, in fisherman's clothes, greeted him from behind a counter piled with small bags of rice. For the tenth time since he had landed he put the question, "Miyamoto Keiko San? . . ." The man did not even bother to answer but, completely disregarding him, went on counting the bags of rice.

Germain went out into the lane. Either Miyamoto has been telling me stories, he thought, or else the whole village is in on the plot. . . . He gave up inquiring, and set off to explore the island. A band of ragged barefoot children followed ten yards behind him. He tried to make friends with the oldest. It was a waste of time, for the minute he turned around they all ran away, straggling back a few minutes later at a respectful distance. The village consisted of three parallel paths along the southern shore of the lake. He went down each of them in turn, carefully, peeping indiscreetly through all the half-open *shoji*. The island seemed to be inhabited by old women and children. Everyone else must have been out fishing. One of the women smiled at him, but most of them hastily closed their *shoji*.

By one o'clock he had visited the entire village, house by house, without finding any trace of Keiko San. He was hungry. He went back to the house where the old woman had smiled at him and found her in her kitchen, beside an oven of fire-blackened earth on which a wooden pot was warming. Pulling two hundred yen from his pocket he showed her by signs that he wanted something to eat. She gently pushed aside the notes, led him into the living room and motioned him to take his place at the low table, with his back to the *tokonoma*. Then, returning to the kitchen, she fetched the potful of white rice and a few small fish that had been grilled in the embers. They ate in silence. He had never enjoyed a Japanese meal so much. There was friendliness in the old woman's gaze. At the end of the meal she poured some green tea onto the remains of her rice and lifted the mixture into her mouth with a swift flick of her chopsticks.

"Gillou San?" she said at last.

He stared at her, amazed to hear his own name. She smiled kindly, took him by the hand and led him into the lane. The gang of children at the door retreated quickly. The old woman shouted something and they fled for good.

"*Massugu,*" she told him, pointing down the lane.

She disappeared into the house, leaving him on the threshold. He went off in the direction she had shown him and soon reached the edge of the village. Further on, she had said. The path ran beside the shore, threading capriciously through the pine trees. After a quarter of an hour's walk he caught sight of three conical straw huts from which white smoke was rising. He heard women's voices and went closer. Inside the huts, around a huge oven surmounted by a caldron, they were engaged in some strange cooking operation. Thousands of shells littered the ground. Germain went into one hut after another, trying to make out faces through the dense vapor. He discovered her in the third hut, bending over the stove as she stoked it with dry wood. She was dressed like the others in a tunic and trousers, with a white scarf knotted around her hair.

"Keiko San," he called gently.

She raised her eyes and looked at him. She showed no sign of emotion.

"Let's go out," she said, "since you've come."

She wiped her hands on her apron and pushed a few stray black locks under her head-scarf. In her boy's clothes she looked tinier than ever.

"You see, I'm making myself useful." She pointed to the shells. "This is the night catch, and they have to be cooked while they're still alive, or else they'd all be wasted. . . . Are you surprised at my dress? All the women here wear nothing else except on feast days. You're in Japan here, in the real unspoiled Japan. No foreigner has ever set foot in this house."

In his overcoat and heavy shoes, he felt ten times more of an intruder. He could think of nothing to say to her.

"Are you happy in Okinoshima?" he asked at last.

"My father loved this island. He often came here for his holidays. I was born here, and as soon as I could walk I wore a tunic and trousers. I'm always happy to come back here."

She answered his questions but made no attempt to keep up the conversation, so that long silences hung heavily between them.

"Keiko San, listen to me. I traveled all night to see you, and tomorrow evening I shall take the plane back to Paris. Before going away I wanted to know."

Her eyes fixed on the lake, she gave him no sign of encouragement, did not even ask what he wanted to know.

180

She only said, "Let's go on a little further."

They sat down side by side on a rock, not far from the huts. They could hear the sound of cheerful voices within.

"I landed on this island at eight this morning, and since then I've been looking for you everywhere."

"I know. They told me at once."

"And you went off to hide in these huts so as to avoid meeting me . . . Keiko San, you did it on purpose. Nobody in the village would tell me anything. But everyone knows you here, your brother told me so. . . ."

A sense of boundless depression swept over him. This unfriendly island, this girl whom he had once held in his arms and loved and who was a stranger now, unrecognizable. . . .

"Everyone knows me, it's quite true—I am almost one of them. A thousand years ago this island was deserted. Then three of Prince Genji's soldiers came to take refuge here, to live unknown and in peace. All the inhabitants of the island are descended from them. People don't care for adventures here. Besides, my cousin had warned them."

"Your cousin?"

"The head fisherman. You saw him this morning, you asked him where I was. It was he that told me."

Germain remembered the disagreeable man who had gone on counting his bags of rice without deigning to answer him.

"But how could you, Keiko San! If I hadn't found you, you'd have let me go on wandering through the island till dark and then leave, without trying to see me again?"

"I am nothing here," she said. "I do what I'm told. Okinoshima is still ruled by the old ways. In Tokyo I am a free agent, I can lead my life as I will, it cannot be otherwise in a modern country. But not here. Here I am only a Japanese girl, meekly obedient to her family, her clan and its customs. If you knew how much more natural it seems!"

"I met one person who didn't think so, an old woman. It was she who gave you away."

"My aunt, my father's cousin."

"I'm glad to see she's cured!"

"Don't be bitter. In Europe, too, there are such things as polite lies."

"You must thank her for me. She's the only person on this island who did not treat me as an enemy."

Once again the girl replied evasively. "She's an incurable romantic!" And she added in a lower tone, "My aunt insisted that if you came, it would mean that you still loved me. Your visit will occupy her thoughts for a long time."

It was his turn now to fall silent, without seeking to confirm the old woman's prediction. Whether he loved or not seemed of no importance here, in this alien land, where there was nothing left for him to do—except go away, forgetting the dream in which he had loved.

"Over there," she said, "on the other side of the water, is Ishiyama, the valley of glowworms. In the old days, lovers whose passion was crossed came there to commit suicide together. . . . That was a long time ago."

The *kami* tree of Nikko, Kanehira, the three soldiers of Prince Genji, the glowworms, the suicides' valley—it was still the dream world. In spite of memories and appearances, he had loved not a real woman but a dream. At his first kiss, his first lover's gesture, he knew, she would vanish through the pines and rocks as though she had never existed.

"Keiko San," he said without looking at her, "I am going away. But first, promise me to answer a question, just one question."

"I promise."

"I think I know why you came to take refuge in this island. Here, you obey—and you obey the power of the past rather than the authority of men. You wanted this island to decide for you, for you lacked strength to decide for yourself. Is that true?"

She slowly bowed her head. "Gilles San," she said so softly that he could hardly hear her, "Gilles San, it would not have been possible."

She went with him as far as the village. They walked in silence along the narrow path, one behind the other. At the first houses she stopped.

"I must leave you now," she said. "From your boat, as you go toward the mainland, look around you carefully. Perhaps you may see some of the beauties of Omi—which is our old name for Lake Biwa—boats making their way back from Yasabe, wild geese flying toward Kataka, or else the sunset over Seta. Perhaps you may hear the evening bell from the temple of Miidera. For the sake of the eight beauties of Omi, thousands of pilgrims used to flock here from all the provinces of old Japan. They waited long and patiently. Alas, you will have no opportunity to see the other four: a snowy evening, a rainy night, a bright sky at Awazu, or the autumn moon over Ishiyama."

The dream still lingered.

"It was considered a wonderful thing to behold a single one of Omi's beauties in a lifetime. If that blessing is granted you, let that be your comfort. You will not have traveled here in vain. . . ."

She gave him a smile of great sweetness, and went away along the path.

He found Kanehira waiting for him at the quayside, gossiping with some women. They stopped talking as he came up. The little harbor became silent. He got into the boat.

"*Otsu,*" he told the fisherman.

"*Hai, hai!*"

The boat sped toward the open sea. An hour later, as the outline of the island grew blurred in the sunset glow, he heard a distant bell.

"Miidera?" he asked.

"*Hai,*" the old fisherman replied gravely. He knew nothing about it. But did it matter? All the vesper bells around Lake Biwa echo over Miidera.

At Haneda, on the following night, April 30th, Germain and his five tourists were about to board the Air-France plane for

183

Paris. A Japanese girl in a kimono was with the party—Miss Prudence, Tomoko San, the maid from the Pine Wind Inn, whom Brownley was taking back to England—as a housemaid, so he said. He was taking his dream home with him.

Mr. Miyamoto, all dignified cordiality, wearing a black jacket and striped trousers for the occasion, lavished regretful farewells. He was loaded with presents and had forgotten nobody. When the loud-speaker in the waiting-room bade the travelers pass along to the departure runway, he offered each of them, with due ceremony, a copy of the *Asahi*—the newspaper whose staff he had joined the previous day, thanks to the kind offices of Sato San.

"Page six," he said, "my article. . . . A tribute to your visit."

Germain held out his hand. The little Japanese clasped it. For all his smile, there were tears in his eyes.

"Did you see Keiko San at Okinoshima?" he asked.

"No," lied Germain, "I couldn't find her."

This time it was he who was saving face.

"She will be sorry for that," said Miyamoto. Then he added: "I am sorry too."

For that moment, he was sincere.

As the aircraft flew over the lights of Tokyo Germain read through Miyamoto's article, in the first edition of the next morning's *Asahi*, dated May 1st:

> Last night, at Haneda Airport, six true friends of Japan took their leave of us. In an interview, the honorable Sato San, of the Tokyo Police, whose efficient authority ensures the safety of foreign visitors to our capital, said: "Among the thousands of tourists with whom I have had to deal I have never before met with such a genuine wish to understand Japan, such an appreciation of our essential problems. I only wish that all honorable visitors from the West may in future model their behavior on that of M. Gilles Germain and his party of tourists." I have lived among them, and I can bear witness to the immense sympathy they have won from those around them, through their tact, their respect

for our customs, their extreme politeness. Toyota San, Prior of the Temple of Z———, which is close to the inn in which these honorable tourists were staying, said to me only this morning . . .

Germain folded up the paper. For his first effort, Miyamoto had really surpassed himself. The comedy was being played out. Nicole Marchand read the article in her turn.

"He's making fun of us in a big way!" she said.

Germain smiled. "I'm afraid you've not understood the first thing about Japan."

The coast was left behind and the plane was rushing through blackness over the China Sea. They went to sleep. . . .

When he reached London two days later Brownley discovered that he needed medical attention. So did Tomoko San.

"You might have warned me!" he told the girl. Covered with confusion, she tittered behind her hand. But the gesture had lost its charm. He kept her until she was cured, then gave her some money and let her go. With her exotic charm she found no difficulty in getting a job in a brothel in Kensington, where she made a great hit with rich, respectable gentlemen. Brownley, still clinging to his dream, visited her two or three times. She always welcomed him joyfully. But the atmosphere was lacking. He missed the gleaming yellow mats, the little lamp in the garden, the delicate *shoji*, the cups of green tea and Mme. Hashi's smile. He soon gave up seeing her.

Miss Angelica Simpson, back home in Burke City, South Dakota, learned of the failure of her mission through a polite, apologetic letter from Sergeant Ogura, which concluded as follows: *I shall try to maintain in your former chapel the earnest piety which you brought to its foundation.* . . . Disgusted with the heathen in general, she listened to the sage advice of her minister, David Wolf, and devoted herself henceforward to local good works, in which she found her hopes rewarded a hundred-fold.

Inspector Ogura, on his promotion, was placed in charge of

the new police station established in the sometime chapel. He stubbornly refused to have the old harmonium removed. He would often play it in the evening, between patrols, working the pedals for all he was worth. His men loved the harmonium. They thought it incredibly amusing.

And how they laughed. . . .